Ladies in Beach Huts

Foreword

Inspired by the 'men in sheds' concept, four friends meet regularly, sometimes in a beach hut, to chat about writing, the dream of being published, winning a competition, seeing their names in print. They knew their writing was competent, sometimes interesting, sometimes funny and enjoyed hearing each other's stories but finding an audience was proving difficult.

So, with nothing to lose, they decided to sift out their best work, produce an anthology featuring their short stories and self-publish.

As they worked together and supported each other, sometimes the themes, or inspiration, for their stories were the same. These stories have been grouped together so the reader can see how different results can be arrived at from a similar starting point.

Right at the end you will find four stories all with the same opening sentence: 'He turned the key in the lock and opened the door. To his horror ...'. See how much those stories differ!

There is no single theme running through this book of short stories in terms of the content, but the authors have enjoyed putting it together and we hope you enjoy it too.

Contents

Farewell Ladies in Beach Huts

By

Shelagh O'Grady

Mavis settled herself into her deckchair outside the beach hut and felt the warm April sun on her face. The padded folding chair which her two best friends had bought for her birthday last month felt very comfortable. She sat quietly for a while listening to the waves breaking on the sand, the sound of children's laughter as they played at the water's edge and the shrill cries of seagulls overhead.

"Joan and Brenda will be along soon. It's such a glorious day for our Tuesday get-together," she thought as she picked up her knitting. Mavis soon had the needles clicking on a baby's shawl for her latest grandchild, which was expected at the end of the month.

Her mind wandered back to when she had first met her friends; it was a long time ago, but time seemed to have flown and now it felt like yesterday. The three women, now in their eighties, often wondered at the reason for their longevity.

Joan had been a teacher at the school where Mavis was school secretary. The two women had become friends straight away, sharing the same love of gardening, reading books by the same authors and having the same quirky sense of humour. Their families had grown up together but now their children had flown the nest and finally they were widows together.

Mavis had known Brenda from their college days, the two of them lodging together and becoming firm friends. Brenda never married and became like a sister to Mavis and a maiden aunt to her and Joan's children.

Mavis thought of the birthdays and Christmas parties the three of them had enjoyed together, and holidays when Brenda had joined her family on trips to Scotland and sometimes to France. "Happy times," Mavis murmured to herself as the needles clicked away.

"That sun is getting quite warm," she muttered. "I must find my sun hat." As she heaved herself out of her chair she felt a little dizzy and grabbed hold of the beach hut door.

"Steady on, old girl, take it easy. Don't want to fall over." She waited until her head cleared before she found her sun hat. Pouring herself a glass of water she took a sip before she returned to her chair.

"The sun must be stronger than I thought. It's usually too much wine that makes me dizzy!" Perching the battered straw hat on her head she picked up her knitting and continued her daydreams as she waited for Joan and Brenda.

A little while later Joan plodded breathlessly towards the beach hut. She saw that Mavis had her head down and appeared to be asleep.

"Snoozing already at this time of the morning!" laughed Joan as she shook Mavis gently by the shoulder. The sun hat slid off and Joan saw the serene face of her friend taking her final doze.

"Oh Mavis!" she gasped, "you've gone first!"

Joan fetched a deckchair and sat down next to her friend. Gently she placed the sun hat back on Mavis's head, then picked up one of her hands. It was still warm and Joan struggled to believe that her friend was dead. The slumped figure looked for all the world as if she was asleep.

"You look so peaceful, what a wonderful way to go," Joan confided to her friend's body. "I hope when my turn comes it will be the same."

After a while Joan took out her phone and rang Brenda.

"Are you on your way?" she asked.

"Yes, next stop is the beach. Is everything OK?"

"Well, no. I don't like to break it to you like this. Mavis must have got here early. I've just got here myself and found her sat in her new chair." Joan paused.

"What's the matter, Joan? Is Mavis OK?"

"She's gone, Brenda! She's dead! Mavis has gone first!"

"Are you sure?"

"Yes, quite sure. You'll see when you get here."

"I won't be long, the bus is stopping now."

Brenda stepped off the bus in a daze. Mavis gone, she couldn't believe it. As she hurried past the beach shop she saw a bucket of brightly coloured toy windmills whirling gently in the breeze. Brenda picked out one, paid for it and hurried as fast as her arthritic hip would let her.

Joan sat Brenda in her chair and whilst Brenda was coming to terms with the death of their friend she boiled the kettle.

"Some coffee for you, Brenda," said Joan gently as Brenda wiped away some tears.

"What are we going to do? Shouldn't we call someone, an ambulance maybe?" asked Brenda.

"We will later, but first we have something to do. Do you remember the farewell boxes we all made?"

Brenda paused. "Oh yes, I'd forgotten about them."

"Well, what better time to open Mavis's than now. We know she's gone so waiting a few minutes longer to call someone won't matter."

"Now I remember, we left them here so that we would all know where to find them," said Brenda. Joan rummaged in a cupboard in the beach hut and came out with a large plastic container. Lifting the lid she revealed three smaller boxes wrapped in pretty coloured paper.

"This one is Mavis's," she said holding up a box wrapped in holly-patterned Christmas paper and tied with a red ribbon. Carefully she placed in onto the table, slid off the ribbon and unwrapped the paper. Lifting the lid Joan looked at the contents.

Several years ago the three friends decided they would like to say farewell to their little group in their own special way. Each had prepared a box to celebrate the end of their life and whoever was left would open it and follow the instructions.

"What's inside, Joan?" asked Brenda, her voice dropping to a whisper. It felt as if they were prying into something very private which belonged to their friend.

Joan lifted out a bottle of sherry and then three crystal glasses which she set on the table. Next came half a dozen pretty glass tea light holders, each containing a little candle. "Always the practical one!" commented Joan with a smile as she pulled out a box of matches. Filling the bottom of the box was a long string of bunting, each triangle being knitted from brightly coloured wool. Brenda gave a chuckle as she remembered how Mavis always had some knitting on the go. Finally Joan lifted out two key rings and a sealed envelope and placed them on the table.

"What an odd assortment," said Brenda.

"Looks like the start of a party to me," chuckled Joan.

"What's inside the envelope? We'd better find out what she has to say."

Joan tore open the envelope and took out a single sheet of note paper covered in Mavis's neat handwriting.

"Read it out," said Brenda buzzing with curiosity.

Joan pulled up a chair beside Brenda and read the letter out loud.

My friends, if you are reading this it follows that I have died, crossed the rainbow bridge as they say. Firstly, I would like to thank you for your friendship through the years. I can't remember how many years, nor do I wish to count. You have become my extended family, more precious because we chose to become friends. For your support and understanding through the difficult times I cannot thank you enough.

In my box you will find some bunting, please hang this around wherever we are. I might be lucky enough to depart at the beach hut! Light the candles and surround yourselves with the pretty lights. There is a key ring with a beach hut fob for each of you, a keepsake as a reminder of all the happy times. Open the bottle of sherry and fill the glasses, one for me too. Toast our long and happy friendship and make sure you finish the bottle before you leave!

Maybe you could sing a song for me; you know how I like "I Do Like To Be Beside the Seaside."

I'll be waiting for you on the other side.

Farewell to you both, Joan and Brenda.

Your good friend, Mavis

Joan and Brenda looked at each other, emotion robbing them of speech.

Slowly Joan stood up, took hold of the bunting and started to drape it around the beach hut and over Mavis's shoulders. Brenda lit the little candles and placed them on the ground around Mavis. Taking one of the grandchildren's beach buckets she filled it with sand and pushed the toy windmill into it. The breeze caught the pretty plastic sails and whirled them around.

"Mavis would have loved the bright colours," she said.

"Spark of genius to bring that. Much better than flowers," replied Joan.

She opened the sherry, filled the glasses and they toasted Mavis. After a refill they toasted each other.

As they were finishing their third glass Brenda said, "We ought to call someone, the ambulance I think."

"OK, perhaps it's time," said Joan as she fished her mobile phone from her handbag.

"Shall we sing before they get here?"

"Yes, I think we'd better. I'm feeling quite merry."

Fuelled with sherry they began to sing, shakily to start with, but soon strains of "I do like to be beside the seaside" drifted across the promenade.

Joan noticed a small crowd of passers-by and dog walkers gathering around.

"Please sing it again," said an elderly man. Joan glanced at Brenda and shrugged her shoulders.

"Once more for Mavis," she said. The two women began to sing again and one by one the crowd joined in. As the song drew to a close they heard the wailing of a siren as an ambulance made its way along the promenade.

"Farewell Mavis, till we met again," said Joan.

Scheming Ladies in Beach Huts

By

Pam Sawyer

She unlocked the doors and opened them wide. The familiar smell, slightly musty, salty, and the crunch of dry sand beneath her feet took her back to her childhood. Caroline had waited a long time for this moment. This beach hut had once belonged to her parents and when it came up for sale recently Caroline wasted no time in putting in an offer. The sale was by sealed tender, so she had a few weeks to wait to see if her offer was accepted.

Now here she was at last on a cold, blustery March day, looking inside for the first time in over thirty years. The keys in her hand, so many memories, some happy, some sad.

Caroline thought it was rather shabby and in need of some serious TLC. As she looked, ideas came to mind as to what she could do with it. The interior needs repainting, she decided. A nice pale aqua blue on the walls would look so much nicer than the dull brown, and a darker shade of blue on the exterior walls. Yes, she could make it look very nice and forget the last time she was here.

She wanted it as a sort of bolthole. Somewhere to sit to sketch and paint. A totally different world from her busy working life.

Caroline had arranged to meet her old school friends here. They needed to talk away from other people and telephones. She arranged four chairs and laid out glasses for the wine.

First to arrive was Brenda, a superintendent in the local police force. Tall, slim and dressed in a smart, grey trouser suit, she embraced Caroline and watched as Caroline took a bottle of wine from a cold box and set it down together with some nibbles. Caroline looks good, she thought, beautifully dressed in cream trousers and a cream and turquoise sweater and looking much younger than her late forties. Brenda was swiftly followed by Annette who worked for HMRC and, last but not least, Josie – mad Josie, always late – editor of the local daily paper. The four of them sat on the old chairs left behind by the previous owners. Caroline opened the bottle of wine.

"Cheers, girls." They clinked their glasses together. Josie laughed. "I feel as though I am in an Enid Blyton story."

"More like Macbeth," Caroline and Annette said in unison.

"This is different." Brenda sipped her wine. "We couldn't afford this in the old days." They all fell silent, lost in their thoughts of that time many years ago.

Breaking the silence, Caroline spoke to Josie.

"Still married to Richard, Josie?"

"Of course."

The others laughed. Richard was Josie's third husband.

"Well, this time it's forever."

More laughter. "I'm sure we've heard this twice before." Brenda patted Josie's arm. "How is Beth? Does she get on with her new stepfather?"

"Beth is sixteen, she doesn't get on with any adult but she would love to use the beach hut, Caroline. How do you feel about that?"

"It's fine with me as long as she leaves it clean and tidy for us. I'm looking forward to doing some sketching and Annette is hoping to bring her laptop and complete her novel."

It had been an unusually long, hot, glorious summer all those years ago. Caroline and her friends spent most of the time at the beach hut. Swimming and fishing from the nearby groyne, occasionally one of the boys would be lucky and would catch bass or flat fish. Just enough for their supper cooked on the small stove in the beach hut. It was a wonderful time for all of them, apart from waiting for their O-level results. The week the results were due, Caroline and Alex, her boyfriend, planned to have a party at the hut.

"It'll be great whichever way it goes." Alex and Caroline were in the hut drinking coffee. He kissed the top of her head. "Caro, don't look so glum, you know you are the brainiest of all of us. We'll have a great party, cheer those who haven't done so well and congratulate the clever ones. I've got my dad to get loads of cider and my mum is setting us up with bread and cheese and crisps. We can get chips from the kiosk across the road. Sorted, right?"

Caroline smiled at him. She adored him, her first real love.

"OK, sorted." She reached up and kissed him.

The day after the party Caroline and her friend Annette went to the beach hut to clear up.

"I had a great time last night, Caro."

"Yep, so did I. I thought the boys were a bit mad going skinny dipping."

"And Kate, don't forget."

"Yes, why did she go?"

Annette sighed, "You know Kate."

A few days later Caroline cycled down to the beach. Alex was working but said he would meet her there later. She fancied some time on her own and had brought her sketch book. Mid week the beach was quiet. As Caroline leaned her bicycle against the beach hut she reached for the key under the paving stone by the door. It was then she noticed the doors were slightly ajar, unlocked. Her first thought was that there had been a break in. She heard a voice.

"Alex?" she called as she opened the doors. There was a scuffle inside as Caroline saw Kate pulling her swimsuit up from around her waist and Alex was sitting on the bench tugging on his swimming trunks.

"Alex? Kate? What's going on?" Neither of them spoke.

Caroline turned on her heel, grabbed her bicycle and pedalled swiftly away. She never went back to the beach hut until the day she walked in as the owner.

The years had passed. Caroline went to university, and she became a successful lawyer, finally setting up her own practice. She became well known for prosecutions of people involved in fraud. She never married.

Alex had married Kate, and Caroline heard they had three children and still lived locally. Alex was the owner of a large car showroom on the edge of town, mostly selling high-end luxury cars. Caroline had found out that Alex was having business difficulties and rumour had it that he was at the centre of a VAT fiddle owing thousands of pounds to HMRC. Josie had heard on the grapevine about Alex. As the editor of the local paper she was often invited to social gatherings. People wanted publicity for their worthy causes or more frequently to publicise aspects of their businesses.

This was the reason for the meeting between the four women. Annette explained she couldn't comment on whether there was any truth in the rumours about Alex, but he had come to the attention of HMRC. Brenda said they would hear something shortly, she couldn't say more at this point.

A couple of weeks after the meeting Josie telephoned Caroline with the news that Alex had been arrested.

He probably wouldn't know that Caroline's law firm had been chosen to lead the prosecution against him. One of her staff would be taking the case, with her help and guidance.

The trial lasted two weeks and Alex was found guilty. As the judge said "take him down", Alex looked up and saw Caroline. He looked pale faced and haggard. He turned to the public gallery where his wife sat, tears streaming down her face. He mouthed "I'm sorry" to her. "So you should be, chum," Caroline thought as she walked away to meet her partner Annette. They were going to choose the paint for the beach hut. Annette was waiting for her in their car. She smiled at Caroline. "How did it go?"

"Perfect result," she said as Annette drove out of the car park.

Ladies in Beach Huts, Old Friends

by

Angie Simpkins

Vera parked the car and, taking the rather full bag out of the boot, she just managed to sit it on her little trolley. She did miss David, but times like this were the worst. Straightening her back, she set off along the promenade, causing other walkers to scatter as she pushed the load ahead of her.

On reaching number 17 she searched the bag for the key, glancing up at the sign above the door – "Mon Repose". David had refused to put the sign in place, "it's only a little, shabby old beach hut" had been his words, "that's far too pretentious." After his death last year, Vera had armed herself with a hammer and nails, and standing precariously on a chair had managed to fix the sign in place. "Well, pretentious it may be, but this little old beach hut is no longer shabby," she said to herself, opening the door to the smart interior. The dresser at the back she had painted a fashionable shade of aquamarine, and the walls a slightly deeper shade. The dresser would not have looked out of place in Mrs Bennet's parlour in "*Pride and Prejudice*" for it was covered with exquisite china, lovingly collected over time from car boot sales, antique shops and various bric-a-brac stalls.

The curtains at the door were the shade of blue of a summer sky, and dotted with a pattern of exotic birds of the kind not seen on this coast, and the effect was enhanced by the addition of delicate gauze curtains which moved gracefully in the gentle sea breeze.

Vera unpacked the bag and stowed it away. She set out the smart green coloured table and chairs and went to fill the kettle. She then took out her knitting and settled down to await Helen's arrival.

"This is an ideal spot for people watching," she thought to herself. Waves of nostalgia washed over her as she watched a young couple walk by, entwined in each other's arms and with eyes only for the other. "She looks about nineteen," thought Helen, "the age David and I were when we met all those years ago at the Palais."

The needles clacked away as the mermaid's tail grew. Alice would love it, Vera knew, and with each stitch she imagined her granddaughter's little body snuggled up beside her while they watched Peppa Pig together. There were many consolations in growing old. Tuesdays and Wednesdays were Vera's favourite days because that was when Terry brought Alice to Vera's house for breakfast, and he often stayed for an hour in the evening when he came to collect her. Vera didn't see much of her son apart from that, although since David had died Terry did manage to visit occasionally and help with things like hedge cutting. Her daughter-in-law, Caroline, worked in London those two days, and the rest of the week she worked from home. Vera felt sorry for young people today, they seemed to demand more from life than she and David had when they were first married, but they had to work very hard to provide it.

"Hello, GanB," cried the little girl, blonde curls bobbing as she flung herself at Vera.

"Oh my! Where did you come from?" laughed Vera as she clutched the small figure to her to prevent her from falling. "Where's Daddy?"

"Here he comes, and Micky," she replied, pointing to the tall young man approaching, pushing a buggy ahead of him.

"Hello, Vera," said Jonathan as he unlocked the beach hut next door. "I'm afraid we're going to disturb your peace this morning. Margaret has had to visit her mother, and I volunteered to bring the children down to the beach."

"It's lovely to see you all," said Vera, "and especially this gorgeous girl," hugging Maisy tightly to her. "I must look in my tin to see if I have any biscuits. You never know, there just may be some there."

"GanB, have you got some biscuits? Is Alice coming today? What are you knitting?"

"Questions, questions," laughed Vera. "Let's look in the tin, and no, Alice is not coming today and I am knitting a mermaid's tail for Alice. Look, here it is. Would you like one?"

"It's beautiful," answered Maisy. "Will I be able to swim in it?"

"No, it's to keep you warm when you are sitting down at home reading, or watching television," said Vera.

"You are too good to her, Vera," said Jonathan. "You're like another Grandma. They are very lucky children. Come along Maisy, let's take Micky down to the sea and see if he likes getting his toes wet."

As the little family made their way to the water's edge, Vera looked up and saw a dear familiar figure walking towards her. Here was Helen, her oldest friend. One hand was occupied trying to hold on to a rather battered old hat, and the other clutched a very old carpet bag. "No-one but Helen would come for a day at the seaside dressed like that," thought Vera affectionately as she stood to greet her old friend.

"My, this is very grand, I must say," said Helen admiringly as she surveyed the beach hut's interior. "You are a one, Vera. Trust you to do it up like a room in one of those glossy magazines you buy."

"You know there's nothing I enjoy more than a bit of interior design. What's it to be, tea or coffee?" as the whistling kettle let them know it was ready.

"Oh, I think I'll have a coffee, please, strong and black. I've brought some iced buns to go with it. Do you remember sneaking out of school and spending our dinner money on iced buns from old Sammy, the baker?"

"Yes, and do you remember the time when old Miss Jenkins caught us?"

"Don't I just? Had to stay behind after school and write 100 lines. Happy days!"

"There's Alf coming along. He's just had to have a new hip, but look at him now. You're walking well, Alf. Your usual?" and Vera got up to make him a mug of tea.

"Aye, missus. I thank you. By George it's good to be able to walk along the prom again," and Alf took the mug and made himself comfortable perching on a stool that Vera provided.

"This is my old friend, Helen," said Vera. "We were at school together."

"Pleased to meet you, ma'am," said Alf, downing his tea. "I'd best move on," and he left to continue his constitutional.

"Hello, Mrs B," shouted the young lad as he whizzed by on his skateboard.

"Come back later, I've made a cherry cake," called Vera to his receding back. "That's Graham. He's a nice lad, about fourteen. Of course, he should be at school now but he's got a few problems at home. Doesn't get on with his step-dad. He often comes by and we have a little chat. I don't know what will become of him, I just hope he doesn't get involved with the group of lads that frequently hang about the amusement arcade. I'm sure they would be a bad influence."

"Oh, Vera. There you go again. You always were a mother hen. You should have been a social worker, not a secretary. Come on. Let's go for a paddle."

The two old ladies removed their shoes and stockings, and laughing like the young women they once were held on to each other as they made their way gingerly across the pebbly beach.

Bake Off, Ladies in Beach Huts

By

Pam Corsie

"Good morning, my love," she smiled at the old girl fumbling with the locks on her beach hut. "Would you like a hand with that?"

"No, thank you. I've got to do it myself. It's getting harder to manage as I get older but I'm not ready to give up yet. In fact, it's the thought of a pleasant morning in the sun at the beach that propels me out of bed in the mornings. I think though I really ought to find something a bit more worthwhile to fill my time."

Emma patted her gently on the shoulder as she turned and continued on her run. She was training for the London Marathon. She had pledged to raise £3,000 for a cancer charity, a figure that was looking more and more distant as the date for the Marathon got closer. She needed to concentrate on identifying fund-raising opportunities during today's training. She considered herself very fortunate that, so far, her family had remained untouched by the dreadful disease. In some ways she saw the £3,000 as a sort of insurance policy covering them all for the foreseeable future. Ridiculous reasoning, she knew, but in the same way that a morning at the beach motivated her Grandma, so raising the cash motivated Emma.

Maggie finally raised the flap and supported it on the open doors of the beach hut. "Phew," she whispered, "that took a while. That flap gets heavier and heavier, lucky it's not too windy. If one of those doors had caught the wind the flap would have knocked me out cold."

"Are you talking to me?" a young man asked as he tried to restrain his excitable dog while addressing Maggie.

"No, I'm talking to myself," she replied and laughed. "It happens when you get to my age!"

"Would you like me to put up your sun lounger?"

"That's very kind of you, but I must do it myself. It's important when you get to my age that you carry on doing things for yourself."

"Right you are, enjoy your day."

As the young man jogged away in pursuit of his lively pooch, Maggie stood, hands on hips, watching him and recalling being able to run. She had never been London Marathon standard but she couldn't run for the bus these days without gasping for breath. Here's Pat, she thought, better get the kettle on. Her sister, leaning heavily on a walking stick, was walking towards the beach hut waving her sun hat in her free hand.

"Good morning, Maggie. Got the kettle on?"

"I have," she replied. "Park your bum on that director's chair. That hip looked pretty painful as you walked along. It'll be easier to get out of that chair than off a lounger."

The sun rose in the sky, fluffy white clouds skittered across in front of it but giving little relief from the heat. After catching up on the family gossip, Maggie and Pat dozed in the sunshine, the gentle breaking of small waves on the shore soothing them and easing them both into a pain-free snooze. Children were playing on the sand, building castles, boats, moats and walls to match that of Hadrian. They were having a lovely time, oblivious to the two gently snoring ladies outside their beach hut.

"Any chance you might wake up and make us a cuppa?"

"I'm not asleep, you cheeky madam, just resting my eyes." Maggie smiled at her visitor. It was Emma, now at the end of her training run, and looking, in Maggie's eyes, as though she could do with something stronger than a cuppa.

"Have a seat, Em," she said. "I'll top up the kettle, won't be long. Pat and I can always find room for another one."

Emma sat on the vacated sun lounger with her head between her knees. "You wanna watch you don't do yourself some damage," muttered Pat. "I used to run but look at me now. Can hardly walk, even with that thing," she pointed to her walking stick, abandoned on the floor next to her chair.

"I'll be careful, Aunty Pat, but I think I've got a few years to go before my hips pack up. Once I've done this run I'll rethink my training programme and take it easy for a while."

"How's the fundraising going?"

"Not bad at all, I've got about £340 to raise to make £3,000. Unfortunately, I'm running out of ideas about how to raise the remaining cash."

"Me and your Gran will think of something," said Pat, "although why you're doing it when there's no-one in our family who will benefit, I don't know." Pat was a firm believer that charity began at home but Emma knew she and Gran would come up with something.

***

"Come on, Maggie, pass me the end of that bunting, I'll pin it over the door then we'll be just about ready." She stood back to admire her and her sister's handiwork. The beach hut looked wonderful. The hand-written signage was a bit tacky but they had wanted it to be a surprise for Emma so they couldn't ask her to produce the signs on her computer. Alice from the beach hut next door came to see how they were progressing.

"Mine's done too," she said. "Come and have a look. Janet has worked very hard." Sure enough, the two beach huts looked amazingly pretty and the old ladies hoped they would draw a crowd. It wasn't long before Maggie and Pat had their first customers.

"How much are the chocolate ones, Miss?" asked a gap-toothed little boy.

"85p each or two for £1.50." He ran off to report back to his mother and get the money and before long the two beach huts were doing a roaring trade in homemade cakes. The young man with the lively dog bought a box of eight assorted cupcakes to take back to the office. He also made a hefty donation as well as paying for the cakes. Several people that the beach hut ladies had given sticking plasters to, shared their beach furniture with and even made a cup of tea for during the hot summer were delighted to repay kindnesses received. They stuffed cash into the collection boxes on the cake tables and bought cakes, told their friends and one even walked up and down the promenade with a tray selling goodies to sunbathers.

The ladies lost count of the times they heard someone say, "Haven't had homemade cake for years." Or, "No-one in my family bakes, I must learn how to do this, these are scrummy." Cake making was clearly a dying art amongst the yummy mummies at the beach.

"What's going on here?" Emma paused on her training run as she drew alongside the gaily decorated beach huts with their queues of people. "Gran, what are you up to?"

"Hello, darling. Can't stop and chat, customers to serve, money to raise. Keep on training, pop in on your way back."

Emma shrugged and set off on her way, smiling to herself. Good old Gran, she thought, or maybe not so old after all, looks as though she found something worthwhile to do after all. Cake making and selling them with her friends, who'd have thought it?

By the time Emma got back to the beach the ladies were just packing away the last of the empty tins, folding up the picnic tables they'd used for a counter. "Where's Gran?" asked Emma.

"In her counting house," laughed Alice, pointing to the neighbouring beach hut.

"Oh Emma," cried Maggie as Emma sneaked up behind her and patted her round bottom. "Look, just look at this." On the tiny beach hut kitchen worktop sat neat piles of coins, lots of neat piles of coins and a stack of notes.

"Gran!"

"Ooh, I know love. Isn't it marvellous. People have been so generous. Lots of donations as well as the money Aunty Pat and I raised from selling cakes. Janet and Alice from next door did well too. All in all we've raised £355 pounds for your London Marathon fund."

"Gran!" Emma burst into tears. "I had no idea, I thought you were doing this to do something worthwhile for yourself not me."

"I'm doing it for myself too, we've had several orders for cakes on a regular basis. That nice young man with the crazy dog came back with a poster he'd done at work to put up in his office advertising our baking company and gave us several more to use to spread the word."

"Baking company? What baking company?"

"Well, the four of us decided we were too young to throw in the towel just yet and as long as we don't get so busy we don't have time to come to the beach we'll be happy. In fact, your Aunty Pat's hip's improved no end since she's had something else to think about."

"I heard that," said Pat and she threw a well-aimed damp cloth in the direction of Maggie's head.

Henry's Present

By

Shelagh O'Grady

"Hi Grandad!" called a cheery voice.

Henry turned, resting on his broom, and saw Steve, his grandson, striding across the grass.

"Thought I'd find you here," said Steve. "You're always sweeping the churchyard paths. This must be the tidiest place in town!"

"'ello, Steve, this is a nice surprise. What brings you 'ere?"

"College finished early today so I'm on my way home. Thought I'd take a short cut through the churchyard and see if you were around."

"That's kind of you, son, sparin' a thought for yer ol' Grandad. 'ave you got time to sit down for a while? My back could do with a bit of a rest."

"Ok, I'm not in any hurry," replied Steve. Henry sank onto a nearby bench, his aching body glad of a break.

"T'is yer Grandma's birthday tomorrow," said Henry.

"So it is, have you got her a present?" asked Steve.

"Yeah I 'ave! I got it t'other day when I were lookin' round a car boot sale," said Henry swelling with pride.

"Not another silver cake slice?" asked Steve.

"No. She got plenty o' them!"

"Electric curling tongs?" queried Steve, teasingly.

"No, no, no! T'is summat nice, to go with 'er best dress!"

"Well, come on then, tell me what you've got!" pressed Steve.

"I found a luvverly emeroid necklace!" purred Henry.

"Haemorrhoid? Are you sure?" asked Steve wondering just what his Grandad had bought.

"Course I'm sure! Emeroids! That's what they be. They match 'er eyes!"

"I never heard of haemorrhoids being made into a necklace, nor matching anyone's eyes!" exclaimed Steve.

"They's big and sparkling, strung together on a silver chain," enthused Henry.

"Haemorrhoids are what you go to the doctors about," protested Steve "They're painful to sit on! They don't make them into jewellery!"

"No, no, not haemorrhoids, EMEROIDS! Beautiful big green stones that shine in the sun! Just like Grandma's eyes. She'll love 'em!"

"Grandad, do you mean emeralds?" asked Steve.

"Yeah! That's what I keeps saying, emeroids!"

"So you did, Grandad," agreed Steve smiling gently. "How is Grandma? Still busy with her garden?"

"She be 'ome right now, fillin' up her tubs for summer," replied Henry.

"What's she planting this year?" Steve's knowledge of plants was sketchy.

"Not too sure. They be pink, an' purple, an' white," Henry paused. "Peculiars I think she said."

"Peculiars? What are they, Grandad? Something new?"

"No, she had 'em last year. Said they was pretty, so she's 'avin' 'em again this year."

Steve scratched his head. "I never heard of plants called peculiars."

"The council puts 'em in baskets down the 'igh street. Hangs 'em orf lamp posts and the like," explained Henry.

"You don't mean petunias, do you?" asked Steve making an inspired guess.

"Yeah, that's what I keep tellin' 'ee. Peculiars!"

"Oh, Grandad!" Steve sighed.

"Her puts big pots of 'em beside the petticoat doors."

"What's petticoat doors, Grandad?" asked a bemused Steve.

"Ain't you got none?" queried Henry. "Them's doors what goes from the sittin' room into the garden. Petticoat doors!"

"I think you mean patio doors."

"Like what I said, petticoat doors! Your 'earin's bad today, Steve. Your mum should get you to the doctors and 'ave your ears checked."

"I don't think it's *my* ears Grandad, but you might have a problem with yours!" Steve chided gently.

"You cheeky young whippersnapper! You watch what you're asayin'!"

Steve grinned and glanced at his watch. "Time I was going Grandad, it was nice to chat," he said getting up to leave. "Wish Grandma a happy birthday from me, and I hope she enjoys her necklace."

"I'll tell 'er," said Henry. "Bye, Steve, nice of you to stop by."

"So long, Grandad." Steve strode off giggling to himself.

"Nice boy, Steve, pity he don't hear so well," muttered Henry as he picked up his broom. "I know his Grandma will love her emeroids!"

A Friend for Life

By

Pam Corsie

The girl with the thick, dark brown hair who was sitting in front of me turned and looked sideways at me over her right shoulder.

"Well," she said, "do you wanna be my friend?"

"Yea, OK," I grudgingly replied whilst, inside, my heart was singing, a friend, a friend who has chosen me.

And that was how it started. Two little girls from council estates, who had miraculously passed the 11-plus test, had found themselves at grammar school, floundering in the company of posh, private-school girls who lived in houses situated in tree-lined avenues. Of course, we would be friends, why ever not?

We lived two bus journeys apart but true friendship does not see that as an obstacle. We stayed at each other's houses at the weekends and in school holidays. We slept top to tail in each other's virginal single beds, giggling, talking and planning. We intended to marry, have families, careers, but would always be best friends. We were going to grow old together.

And thus it continued. As our lives progressed, there were times when we didn't see each other for weeks on end, especially when our children were small and we were busy trying to "have it all". What an awful eighties expression! But we stayed in touch by the miracle of the telephone and tried to spend birthdays together, with our husbands who had also become friends. Four times a year we ate lavish dinners in posh restaurants with sumptuous puddings washed down by many bottles of wine and accompanied by raucous laughter at our husbands' off-colour jokes.

As our children grew and no longer needed constant supervision we got our lives back. Many nights out with husbands and friends, girls' nights out with just each other and, of course, an annual holiday, no husbands, or kids, allowed!

We were brilliant at laying on a beach in the sunshine, reading and swapping books, chatting about anything and everything. As we people-watched from pavement cafés, we'd spot old ladies in beige cardigans, arm-in-arm, propping each other up, as best friends do, tottering along various promenades in the sunshine, clearly having a lovely time.

"That'll be us before we know it," we'd say. "The White Hair and Walking Sticks Tour, we'll call it." How we would laugh at the thought.

We began to notice the changes as middle age rapidly approached. It became harder to leap off the sunbed and into the pool. More of a sort of "Humph, urgh, I'm up!"

"Do you think I am getting more freckles, or are these age spots?"

"I've got a permanent pain under my ribcage, that's not right is it?"

"Perhaps your bra is too tight, you're not the size 10 you were!"

And that was how it continued. A lot of banter, followed by concern and then an endless stream of GP appointments, tests in the, hitherto unvisited, mysterious rooms in the hospital, and, finally, an appointment with a consultant.

"How did you get on?" I asked on the phone that evening.

"It's not great, in fact it couldn't be worse," Sue sobbed. It had to be bad, we were not the sort of friends that wept over each other normally. We had more of a "things happen, have a glass of wine and get over it" friendship.

"Well, if it is something horrid, at least you are being looked after and the sooner you are treated, the sooner you'll get better. You'll be fine, don't worry." The eternal optimist, that's me!

"You're not listening," she said wearily. "I've got a shadow on my lung, on both lungs, in fact." Even I couldn't be optimistic about that horrible news. "I've got to have an MRI scan."

And so it carried on. The MRI scan revealed advanced cancer of the pancreas, untreatable. She was given six months to live.

"We need to go on the White Hair and Walking Sticks Tour right now," she smiled when we wiped our eyes. "Any ideas?"

"Loads." I sniffed, "Give me a few hours and I'll come up with a plan."

Clearly we couldn't go far because of fitting in doctor's appointments, chemo dates and it was, of course, dependent on what Sue felt able to do. Luckily, we live in beautiful Dorset and in the summer there is plenty to do. I soon had a plan of outings, stately homes, National Trust gardens, landmarks and, of course, several visits down memory lane to places we had grown up alongside.

Chemo was Mondays, Tuesdays she was too tired to do much, but by Wednesdays things were better and we embarked on the White Hair and Walking Sticks Tour, about 15 years earlier than we wanted to, but it had to be done. One day, as we strolled through the gardens at Abbotsbury Swannery, Sue remarked, "The flowers are so beautiful, the colours so vibrant and the baby swans are gorgeous."

"What's come over you, waxing lyrical? What's happened to cynical Sue, my best friend? This is not like you."

"No it's not, is it? Ever since I found out about, you know, I've seen things differently. Stuff that I would normally take for granted is brighter, more alive, more beautiful."

"Does that include me?" I asked with a grin.

"Ha ha. No. Only things I look at and don't know too much about. I know far too much about you to be fooled into thinking you're bright and beautiful. Although, as best friends go, you're not too bad!"

So, not completely lost her cynicism or sense of humour.

The phone rang. "Hi, it's only me," she said. "On Monday I've got my last chemo for a few weeks. I don't suppose you fancy going to Pisa on Wednesday for a few days, do you?"

"I most certainly do." I replied. "Are you going to be up for this?"

"The White Hair and Walking Sticks Tour goes abroad! Of course, I'm up for it."

So that's what we did. We took the tour, all two of us, to Pisa, where we stayed in a beautiful old building that had been a nunnery in a former life. As we lay in our virginal single beds on that first night, we reminisced about other nights, many years ago, when we had shared a single bed in our teenage bedrooms and the Beatles looked down from the walls and listened to us making plans.

Through some unseen, but unsurprising, surge of strength, willpower, stubbornness, call it what you will, Sue rallied each morning from a drug-induced sleep and was raring to go. We breakfasted in a sunny courtyard with other guests and then ventured out. We walked up to the leaning tower and took silly photos of each other pretending to push it into an upright position. We went to Florence on the train and oohed and aahed our way around beautiful buildings and famous works of art. We took a bus to Lucca and hired bicycles so we could cycle, albeit fairly slowly, atop the walls of the town. We stopped periodically to admire the view of the village. White painted houses, winding alleys, small sunny squares and lots and lots of geraniums and bougainvillea trailing from balconies and window boxes. We laughed and laughed as we wobbled along. We stuck out our legs and cruised on the down slopes. We pretended we were two of Enid Blyton's Famous Five, books we had both loved when we were children, getting up to high jinks and waving our bottled water in the air. "Lashings of ginger beer," we giggled, much to the amusement of other cyclists.

Eventually we completed the circuit and returned the bicycles. We sat in the sunshine, sipping Chianti alternately with ice-cold water and recalling other cycle rides, taken as teenage girls – to the beach, the local caravan park, the shops, to the homes of other friends. And we laughed, not only at our own exploits but also at some of the more ungainly, wobbly riders who were also mad enough to hire bicycles in Lucca in the heat of the day.

On our return to the UK Sue was very tired. "The price to pay for a lovely holiday," she explained. "But it was worth it." We continued the tour as before on days when Sue was well enough. Another round of chemo was endured and fourteen months after her diagnosis she was showing signs that the cancer was winning. Despite the chemo, the steroids and a will of iron, Sue was beginning to fade in front of my eyes.

She became quite reluctant to go out. She didn't complain but I could see in her face that she was in a lot of pain, pain made worse by simply moving around. The White Hair and Walking Sticks Tour was reduced to coffee in the park or half a lager on the quay in the sunshine. Finally the tour was completed. We had nowhere else to go except back to the local hospital and then to a hospice where Sue finally fell asleep forever.

It was 48 years since she first asked if I wanted to be her friend. I am so glad I said yes, so glad to have known her, to have had her company since I was 11. Her sense of humour, her cynicism, her honesty and her loyalty all enriched me. She was my best friend, I loved her, and, several years later, I still miss her every single day.

The Garden

By

Pam Sawyer

"What have you been doing while I have been away?"

Christine looked at her husband, sitting in his favourite armchair. His long legs stretched out in front, fair hair bleached almost white by the desert sun and his face tanned, although he had gained a few more lines around his eyes and mouth since she last saw him. Six long months ago.

"Come with me, and I will show you." She held out her hand to him, together they left the house and walked down to the road and followed the path around the football field.

"Chrissie, where are we going?"

"It's not far now," They went through a gap in the hedge, and there before Tom was the most delightful garden. "What on earth?"

"When you all went away Jenny and I had this idea, we thought it would be good to create a small garden, somewhere where we could sit, grow a few veg and flowers."

He looked around at the profusion of flowers and neat rows of vegetables, a small grassy area with a sand pit and a few children's toys.

"Well this isn't a small garden, it would rival the size of my Grandad's allotment and how did you get permission? This is MOD land after all."

"Yes I know, but you know how persuasive Jen can be. She spoke to Staff Sergeant Ransom, and he said he would sort it, and sort it he did. He even got a couple of lads to give us a hand clearing the land."

"Hmm, Jim Ransom was always easily moved by a pretty face." They walked the length of the plot, stopping now and then to look at some of the flowers and vegetables. Tom leaned over and touched a small shrub. "This is nice, what is it?" "It's Rosemary," she hesitated. "For remembrance." A shadow passed across Tom's face.

He moved along to the wooden bench and sat down patting the bench. "I suppose Jim procured this as well?"

"No, we were very lucky when news went round about what we were doing; lots of folk donated stuff, mostly the civilian staff or the wives who had jobs and the camp maintenance people lent us tools which saved us quite a bit. We also had help from several of the mums who were not working. They would come and bring their babies and toddlers. So we set aside an area for the children to play and grow things like the sunflowers and tomatoes.

"We also had cake sales to raise cash for things like compost, although we got the kitchens organised to give us suitable waste and soon had our own compost heaps. They are over there behind the small fenced-off bit." She pointed to two neat, wooden constructions. "Our compost heaps, they will be ready for next year," she said with a smile on her face.

"This certainly is a nice peaceful place, I can't believe what you have achieved, I never realised you had green fingers."

"Neither did I," Christine laughed. "It kept us busy and helped to take our minds off what you were coping with." They sat close together and silent for a while.

"About Marcus..." Christine looked at Tom, he had closed his eyes.

"Chrissie, I can't talk about it, he was my best friend, and we were closer than if we had been brothers."

"I'm sorry, but I felt so sad and knew how hard you would take his death, I wanted so much to be able to comfort you, I was very lonely when Jenny left and went back up to Scotland to be with Marcus's family. I really miss her." Tom took her hand and raised it to his lips.

"Jenny and I went to Wootton Bassett to be there when Marcus and the others came back. It was very moving and the people were so kind."

"Don't, Chrissie, please."

Tom stood. "Let's go back, I am very impressed with the garden, but I would really love a proper cup of tea. I am on leave shortly so let's go and make a few plans. One thing I would like is to go and see Marcus's parents. I have letters from Marcus for them and Jenny and I would like to give them in person, and if it's OK with you, we could make a trip to Scotland as part of my leave."

Christine leaned towards Tom, linked her arm with his and thanked her lucky stars he had come back safely, although she realised he was very much changed from the rather carefree man who had marched away all those months ago.

Arm in arm they walked back to their house, both deep in their own thoughts.

Albert's Christmas

By

Angie Simpkins

The old man muttered to himself as he rubbed a piece of rag across the black cake in the tin, and began to rub hard on his boots.

"It's a few years since I've had to do this," he thought to himself. "I wonder what became of the old crowd. I know poor old Terry fell off his perch, and Micky ended up doing time at Her Majesty's Service, not the sort of time we all did when SS Uganda ended up in that Godforsaken place. Charlie did alright for himself, got a job in his father-in-law's garage and lived in a nice little house, again courtesy of Brenda's dad, but paid a price – had to live with Brenda. Miserable old woman she turned out to be. Me, what have I got to show for all the years I served my country? Bugger all, that's what! Never mind, things seem to be picking up now."

"Albert. Are you ready?" called the young woman from the bottom of the stairs.

"Nearly, me old duck," replied Albert, peering over the banister at Molly, standing in the hall of the hostel.

"Have you had any breakfast?" asked Molly. "I've got two cups of tea here, and a bacon sandwich. Shall I come up?"

"You'd better not let the old dragon see you then," said Albert, his mouth watering at the thought of a bacon sandwich. He knew Molly would have bought it from Tariq's van, and, surprisingly for a Muslim, Tariq made the best bacon sandwich Albert had ever tasted.

Molly sat on the bed and watched contentedly as Albert devoured the sandwich. She had grown rather fond of the old soldier and it had upset her to think of how he had been homeless on and off for twenty years, after leaving the army.

"Have you heard from your Maureen lately?" she asked.

"Not a word since Christmas three years ago," came the reply. "I suppose I'm a grandad now, but I don't even know if I've a grandson or a granddaughter."

"Which would you rather have – a grandson or a granddaughter?" asked Molly.

"Either, I wouldn't mind. I'd just like to get to know him or her."

"Well, your lifestyle has made it pretty difficult for Maureen to contact you, hasn't it? You never know, the Salvation Army may have some luck in tracing her. They're very good at that. I have a good feeling about this. Keep hoping, perhaps this Christmas will be the one. Anyway, it's time we went. Come along."

They went downstairs and out onto the street. The day was bright, but crisp and cold. Albert pulled the collar of his old coat up. "It's not far," said Molly, "just along here. I'll drive you as it's your first day."

"How am I supposed to fit in this," said Albert with dismay, surveying the small, yellow car.

"Oh, come on, you'll manage," said Molly as she held the door open for him and took his elbow to guide him back onto the seat.

"I feel like a bloody sardine in a tin," grumbled Albert as Molly eased the car into the traffic. They pulled up outside the back entrance of Hancock's, the biggest department store in the town.

Molly came round to the passenger side to help Albert extricate himself from the car.

"I didn't know it was here," said Albert. "Bit posh ain't it?"

"You'll be just fine," reassured Molly. "Look at you, you're perfect for the part."

They entered the store, and Molly led Albert to the lift, where they alighted on the top floor. She knocked on one of the doors and, on being invited to enter, she introduced Albert to a smart young man wearing a suit, shirt and tie. "This is Albert," she said. "Albert, this is Jeremy. He'll look after you."

Jeremy stepped forward and held out his hand, "Very pleased to meet you, Albert. Have you done this work before?"

"Never," replied Albert.

"Well, don't worry. I'm sure you'll be fine. You are certainly the right build. I don't expect you to be too busy today and by the weekend you'll be in the swing of things. I'll take you to change into your uniform."

Jeremy led Albert to a clean and functional restroom and pointed to a box on the table. "It's all in there," he said. "I'll pop back in 10 minutes in case you need a hand with anything."

Albert gingerly opened the box and took out a large pair of baggy black trousers and a large red coat with a soft white fur trim. He took his shabby old clothes off and pulled on the trousers, which were held up by a slim leather belt. "Better than the string I usually use," chuckled Albert to himself. He then donned the red coat and put his shiny black boots back on. He was admiring his reflection in the mirror when Jeremy returned.

"My, don't you look the part?" Jeremy cried with enthusiasm. "You don't even need to stick on the false beard, I should imagine it's very uncomfortable. Give me a 'Ho-Ho-Ho'."

Albert cleared his throat and obliged.

"Perfect," laughed Jeremy, "now, let's go and show Molly."

When Molly saw him, her eyes shone. "Albert, you look wonderful. You make me feel that Christmas is here. We've just got to go through a few things. You know you must not touch the children, without their mothers' permission. Sometimes a child will ask to sit on your lap and that's OK if Mum says it is. The usual patter is to ask what they have asked for for Christmas and have they written to you? If they say yes you must pretend to have received the letter. Then, of course, you ask if they have been good. They might ask questions about your reindeer, especially Rudolph, and some might be concerned how you will deliver the presents if they don't have a chimney. You will have to think of what to say. Some little ones might be nervous and you will just have to let their mother (or father or grandparent) answer for them. You will have an elf to help you (in fact, this afternoon that will be me!), and at the end of the visit you will give each child a gift. Don't worry about that, the elf will hand it to you. The grotto is in the toy department. Melanie – your elf this morning – will take you there, and when you come out of the lift, you should walk through the toy department to your grotto ringing this bell and perhaps the occasional "Merry Christmas everybody" or "Ho-Ho-Ho" would be a good idea. Good luck."

Albert sat back in his chair, taking it all in. "I don't even care about the money," he thought, "although there's no doubt it will be very useful. I think this is going to be a very jolly Christmas."

A Christmas Story

By

Pam Corsie

Clang! Anna glanced up to thank the do-gooder who had dropped a coin into her nearly empty tin. "Cheers, mate." A measly quid, she thought. I bet he's going home to a warm house, twinkly lights, the smell of warm mince pies and mulled wine. Happy bloody Christmas.

Clang! Clang! Clang! "Thanks, love," she smiled at the sad-faced young woman who had dropped three two pound coins. Anna took them out and surreptitiously slid them into the inside pocket of her filthy, scruffy parka with rest of her haul. It didn't do to let the punters know just how much you'd been given. Another one, doubtless off home to a "Hello, darling, I've opened the champagne," welcome. She looked the type who would have a man waiting for her in a brightly lit kitchen, wearing an apron.

Anna hugged the threadbare blanket around her shoulders and tried to keep warm. She had to drag this Christmas Eve out as long as she could when Joe Public was at his most generous, or guilt-ridden, but be ready to leave long before the pubs turned out when she might be kicked, sworn at, spat on or, worst of all, be rumbled and her hard-earned cash stolen. She really needed the money, she had things to buy, preparations to make and, more than that, she really needed to find a permanent home.

The evening slipped by, the inside pocket was feeling heavy. Anna was frozen stiff but determined to remain in this prime position between the underground entrance and the trendy bars and expensive flats to her left. Joe Public had been generous to a fault. Aside from money, she had received a burger and chips, two cups of hot chocolate and a lump of fruit cake. The money was most useful and she was grateful; after all, she could go to the homeless shelter for food. However, deep within her, indignation and pride battled with each other not to surface as well-meaning passers-by dropped their change into her tin, often barely glancing at her, their generosity making her feel invisible, worthless. One guy, in a sharp suit and those pointy shoes favoured by estate agents, dropped a £10 note. It could have been litter for all he cared, but she snatched it up and sat on it until he had gone on his way, not too proud now and a little scared that he had dropped it accidentally and might want it returned.

It was approaching nine thirty when Anna decided to call it a day. Joe Public had been drinking in the bars with his friends since finishing work early on this festive evening. She wanted to be long gone before he prowled the streets searching out other entertainment. She was bent over, stuffing her meagre possessions into a 'bag for life'. The irony, she thought, this is my life, in a bag. A tear trickled slowly down her grimy cheek. She heard someone say, "Come on, gal, pull yourself together," and then shrugged as she realised she was talking to herself. Why would anyone else talk to her? She was invisible.

"Would you like some help with that?"

Who said that, she thought? It wasn't me, was someone else actually speaking to me? She peered up through the bedraggled fur on her parka hood. "No, thank you," she didn't want to risk losing her swag now.

"Do you have somewhere to go? It is Christmas Eve, after all? Is there somewhere I can give you a lift to?"

"Who are you, the Christmas Fairy?" Anna snarled at her new companion. "I saw you earlier," she said. "What are you doing still out? I thought you were on your way home to Mr Perfect."

"Mr Perfect? Does he exist?"

"Obviously not for me, but I really thought he did for you."

"He did once, at least I thought he was perfect until he proved otherwise. He ran off with my best friend about two months ago. It coincided with Halloween. I like to think of her on a broomstick with a mangy cat on her shoulders."

"And him?"

"I don't like to think of him at all. Anyway, enough of that rubbish. I just thought, spirit of goodwill and all that, time of year, nothing else to do, I could help you. My name is Kate. Would you like me to take you somewhere?"

"If only I had somewhere to go. I could go to the shelter with the other scumbags, wastrels and invisible people, but I can walk there."

"Don't say that, not everyone thinks of homeless people like that. I'm sure there are all sorts of reasons why some people don't have a roof over their head."

"You're right, of course. I'm just a bit wary of do-gooders, it's never enough. People who don't have basic warmth and shelter need more than one act of kindness to get them back on their feet. You could drop me at the shelter and I might get some soup, a mattress and a blanket for the night but tomorrow I'll be back here. I have nowhere else to go!"

Kate stared at Anna and, for a split second, knew that if she hadn't had the upbringing she'd had, the education and well-paid job that followed, perhaps their roles would have been reversed. Perhaps she would be on the streets now that Mr Perfect had vanished.

"You could have somewhere to go, if it suits. You could come home with me. I'm rattling around in a house I used to share with Mr Perfect, alone on Christmas Eve. I have an M&S Christmas Dinner for two in the fridge and no-one to share it with. What do you think? Will you join me?"

Anna slowly turned her head. "Okay," she said, "if it stops you feeling lonely and sorry for yourself. I'll go with you. But, no funny business and I'm not paying for an M&S dinner. The soup at the shelter is free and it's homemade."

The two young women walked past the open doors of the bars, wafting in warmth, the smell of food and alcohol and listening to the sound of raucous enjoyment. Kate turned down a side road and about five houses from the corner opened the shiny white door of a mews house. Once inside she gestured to the stairs. "Guest bathroom at the top on the left, if you want to freshen up," she suggested. "There's plenty of hot water if you would like a bath. That always warms me up whenever I get cold."

"Thanks," Anna grunted, "bet you're glad I agreed. I can smell me and I'm used to it. I bet the only reason you're not holding your nose and retching is because you're so posh. Have you got any bubble bath?"

"Of course, help yourself."

It was a good hour later when Anna, sweet-smelling, smiling, wrapped in a dressing gown she'd found on the back of the bathroom door, entered the kitchen where Kate was just about to serve a late supper. "Hi," she said. "I am guessing you're hungry."

"I'm always hungry," Anna replied. "That smells good."

"Fresh crusty bread and homemade soup. I didn't want you to feel you'd missed out on your homemade soup!" Kate raised her eyes from the pan she was stirring, smiling, struggling to recognise the pale-skinned Anna on the other side of the breakfast bar. "We'll eat in the kitchen, it's more cosy. Festive glass of wine to help it down?"

"Oh, no. Not for me."

"Oh, sorry, I didn't think. I don't suppose you want me to have one either, do you?"

"I don't mind. I'm not a drunk, never have been, nor have I done drugs. I'm just not drinking at the moment."

As Anna levered herself onto the bar stool Kate spotted her swollen abdomen under the dressing gown. "Oh, my word, is that what I think it is! Is that why you don't want wine? Is that a baby bump?"

"Yeah, do you want me to leave now?"

"Good heavens, no, of course not. When is the baby due? Where's the father? Do your parents know you are walking the streets in this condition?"

"Soon, dunno, probably but they don't care. I don't want to talk about it if you don't mind."

"If you say so. Let's have our soup, do you want butter on the bread?"

Later that evening Kate showed Anna to the comfort of her guest room. They'd chatted as if they were old friends and the time passed quickly. They had made a plan to go to social services as soon as they re-opened after Christmas to get help for Anna. They found they shared a dry sense of humour, with a hint of cynicism, and agreed that Mr Perfect was the invisible person in their lives.

As she pulled the covers up around her ears Kate found that she was looking forward to Christmas Day, not dreading it as she had been. She was not prepared for the scream that came from her guest room: "Kate, help, the baby, it's coming! Now, it's coming now!"

After the baby girl was safely delivered by the Emergency Community Midwife, Anna and Kate each sipped a flute of champagne, laughing and toasting each other as the irony of a homeless, unmarried woman having a baby in a stranger's house on Christmas morning dawned on them.

Bethany's Christmas Gift

By

Shelagh O'Grady

Sitting on the window seat in her bedroom late one winter's night Bethany watched the snow covering everything in a thick, white blanket. She loved the snow and was fascinated by the huge, lacy snowflakes drifting down from the heavens.

Her restless mind refused to settle and her crippled leg ached, reminding her of all the things that she used to enjoy, tobogganing, building a snowman, a snowball fight and generally having fun. Tears pricked her eyes as she remembered when things weren't like this, when she could run and play like other little girls.

Bethany remembered when she was six years old, the time of the dreadful accident. She was in the car with Mummy and Daddy one stormy night when the rain was sheeting down. Daddy was driving and finding it hard to see the road. Bethany remembered the bright lights and hearing her mother cry out. She remembered the huge bang. Then there was nothing until she opened her eyes and found herself in hospital.

The car had been hit by a large lorry and was badly damaged, causing severe injuries to Bethany and her mother. But her beloved Daddy was... she still couldn't bring herself to say it. Dead was such an awful word! She banged her fist on the seat and tears of anger and despair rolled down her cheeks.

Daddy had been her world. She had idolised him and he had doted on her. He used to take her swimming, taught her to ride her bicycle, and in the swing park he would push her high into the sky and make her squeal with delight. There were times when she rode on his back as he galloped round the garden pretending that he was a horse. Those wondrous, carefree days had gone.

Her mother's injuries had healed but Bethany was left with a deformed leg and she needed crutches to walk. She was ten years old now and this would be the fourth Christmas without her father.

"Why did Daddy have to … die?" she sobbed miserably.

For a while she stared out into the darkness, idly watching the huge snowflakes drifting past the window. As she watched she became aware of a glow amongst the trees down in the garden. Her eyes strained to see who could be out there at this late hour but could see no-one. Rubbing away the tears she looked again and sure enough the glow was still there. She watched it move to the edge of the trees and start to turn pink. Bethany was entranced.

"What is it?" she wondered, her tearful mood vanishing. Opening the window she leaned out to get a better view. The glow increased and more colours seemed to be swirling around. Faintly she heard a noise like the tinkling of a wind chime being blown in the breeze. The snow eased a little and Bethany sat and watched, captivated by the magical scene.

Suddenly she knew she had to find out what it was. Slipping into her dressing gown and slippers, she grabbed her crutches and opened her bedroom door. All was quiet in the big old house except for the ticking of the grandfather clock in the hall. Carefully she made her way to the top of the stairs. The noisy stair lift might wake her mother so she decided to walk down.

"This might be a bit tricky," she thought. Pushing one of her crutches through her dressing gown belt like a sword she grabbed hold of the bannister. One hand held the rail, the other her second crutch, and with great care she descended the stairs. Arriving safely at the bottom she felt a great sense of achievement.

Groping her way through the darkened sitting room Bethany drew back the heavy curtains and opened the patio doors. In the trees across the lawn the light was still shining and it appeared to be getting brighter. A gust of frosty air touched her face making her gasp a little as she stepped out into the garden. The crisp snow crunched under her slippers as she walked across the lawn. She was fascinated by the beautiful light and the little tinkling sound.

Suddenly she stopped and stared. Within the light a figure appeared, someone she recognised.

"Daddy?" she whispered, trembling a little, "Daddy, is that you?"

"Hello, Bethany," replied the figure. "Yes, it's me."

Bethany stood rooted to the spot, not sure she could believe what she was seeing. It looked and sounded like her father but how could it be? He was … dead, wasn't he?

"Are you an angel?" she whispered.

"Yes, I suppose I am," replied her father, smiling at his daughter's puzzled expression. "Let's sit on the bench and we can talk."

Sitting beside her father Bethany asked hesitantly "Can I … cuddle you?"

"I'm afraid not, my darling. I only appear to have a body so that you can recognise me. But sit closer and you will feel how much I love you." Bethany shuffled up the bench nearer to her dad and the glowing light encompassed her too. She was aware of a feeling of warmth and happiness, and gradually realised that this was how she had felt when she was with her dad before that dreadful night. Looking into her father's smiling face she felt tears pricking her eyes.

"Bethany, I've been watching you and have seen how unhappy you are. This makes me very sad. Because of this I have asked for special permission, just for tonight, to return to Earth to see you."

"Has God let you come to see me?" she asked in amazement.

"Yes," Daddy replied. "He is worried about you."

Bethany thought about this. God knew all about her and how unhappy she was! Yet He had left her with a crippled leg. That didn't seem right.

"Why has God given me a bad leg?" she asked.

"I don't know, darling," replied her father, "but I can tell you that it will get better when you start smiling again. It's time to put away all those bad memories, time to start having fun and being happy again."

"But things aren't the same without you, Daddy," sighed Bethany.

"That's true," agreed her father, "but you still have Mummy. She has a broken heart just like you. Together you can help each other to find happiness again. That would make me very happy. I would so love to hear you both laughing again, telling each other jokes and enjoying life. Do you think you could do that for me Bethany?"

"I could try," she replied hesitantly.

Her father continued. "When you feel sad, remember tonight. Imagine this lovely pink glow and feel it in your heart. My love will be with you forever, my precious daughter." Bethany didn't know what to say, and again her eyes filled with tears.

"Did you mean it when you said my leg will get better?" she asked, mopping her eyes on the sleeve of her dressing gown.

"God's message to you is that you must start to laugh and enjoy life again, and then your leg will begin to mend."

"He said that? He really said that?" exclaimed Bethany in amazement.

"God's honour," said Daddy, and they both laughed.

Father and daughter sat on the bench talking and laughing long into the night.

Next morning Bethany's mother found her fast asleep on the sofa in the sitting room. When the extraordinary tale of the night before was recounted mother and daughter hugged each other knowing that at last their lives could move forward.

After the happiest Christmas she had experienced for years, Bethany began to smile again, especially when she remembered that special night. The happiness drew her closer to her mother and they found support in each other.

Slowly the miracle began to happen and one summer's day Bethany found that she no longer needed her crutches. Going into the garden she sat on the bench.

"Thank you, God," she whispered. "Thank you for keeping your promise."

The Visit

By

Pam Sawyer

The young man stood quietly by the open gates, he looked down the drive and, taking a few steps inside, he paused and looked at the house. He watched his family through the windows, as although it was completely dark the curtains were still open. His father stood and raised a glass to the people sitting round the table, his sister, her husband and their children. His father put down his glass and started to carve a large turkey. His mother appeared with two dishes filled with vegetables and set them on the table.

As he watched, his stomach rumbled reminding him that he hadn't eaten since yesterday, when he left the hostel. He looked down at his ripped jeans and scruffy shoes. It had been a mistake to come here. He walked out of the gate, down the lane to the road where, seeing the lights from a pub, he crossed the road and went inside. It went quiet as everyone turned to look at him. From a canvas holdall he took a couple of Big Issue magazines. "Big Issue anyone?" he said. Nobody spoke. A man hurried from behind the bar.

"Look here, son. What do you think you are doing?"

"I haven't any money and I thought if I flog a couple of these," he pointed to the magazines, "I could perhaps buy a sandwich."

"Well, think again and clear off, we don't want your sort in here."

A woman tugged at his sleeve as he turned towards the door.

"Come and sit here." She pointed to a small table by the fire. "I can make you a sandwich, there is turkey left from lunchtime and some ham." A lump formed in his throat as he remembered the family sitting down to their meal.

"But I cannot pay."

"Don't worry about that, it's on the house, isn't it, Frank?"

While he waited, he played with a box of matches which had been left on the table.

The woman returned with two rounds of sandwiches, one turkey, one ham. He thanked her. "Would you like some Christmas pudding and custard after that?"

"Thank you, if it's not too much trouble."

"Frank, get this young man a drink."

Frank glared at his wife. "Okay, okay."

Finishing his food, he picked up his plates and glass and returned them to the bar. He grabbed his holdall and rucksack and reluctantly left the warmth of the pub.

He returned to his parents' house just as his sister and her family were leaving. Hiding in a hedge he watched them drive off. He took a Big Issue out of his bag and walked to the front door. Lighting the magazine, using a match from the box on the table at the pub, he pushed it through the letterbox.

Minutes later, as he walked down the road, he smiled as a fire engine raced past him with its blue lights flashing.

"Yes!" he shouted punching the air with his fist.

The Gene Editor

By

Angie Simpkins

The unusually empty laboratory caused Richard a moment of reflection. How long had he spent in this oh-so-familiar environment? The humming of the machinery he had always found vaguely soothing, and the order and pristine condition of the work surfaces and equipment was satisfying. Today was his birthday, but his colleagues were unaware of this, and certainly unaware of the number of years he had behind him.

"Hi buddy," came from the young man who burst enthusiastically through the door. "Have you heard yet?"

"Not yet, Freddie. The decision should be made by lunchtime today and we expect an announcement tonight," replied Richard.

"What does Maggie think of it, is she keen to go too?" asked Freddie.

"She was the one who put our names forward," answered Richard. "We're meeting up with the other applicants this evening, and the final decision will be taking into account how we get on with each other."

"That's you off the list then," joshed Freddie.

"If you don't mind, I'm going to call it a day now," said Richard. "I've a few things to do before tonight."

As the transporter took him home he reflected on the past 150 years. He and Anna had been working together way back in 2015 and were part of the team who had discovered gene therapy. They had managed to edit certain genes and thus found a cure for many previously fatal conditions. He thought back to that fateful weekend when just he and Anna had worked alone in the laboratory, and had succeeded in discovering what they thought was the gene which caused ageing. In their youthful enthusiasm they decided to experiment on themselves, and the result was that now here he was, 150 years later, in the year 2166, alone with the consequences of their youthful folly. After ten happy years together the love of his life, Anna, had left to take up a job in a laboratory in California, and on a flight to give a lecture in

Boston her plane had crashed. There were no survivors. There had been other relationships over the years, and heartbreak in some cases when his lovers had inevitably grown older and he had been forced to leave lest his secret be discovered. He had never found anyone with whom he felt he could share his secret, knowing that he was destined to outlive them. Now he had to make a big decision. Would he join the exploratory space probe together with Maggie and whoever else was selected, and risk being left isolated on an alien planet? Perhaps they would not be chosen, and he would not have to make the decision. Maggie was the instigator, and would be very disappointed if they were not chosen. Maggie was special, and there were times when he had considered telling her the truth, but those moments had passed.

His transporter arrived at the door to their apartment. He alighted, removed his sunglasses to look at the iris identifier pad, and as the door opened he was greeted by Maggie handing him their usual cocktail – a concoction of alcohol created in a laboratory somewhere in the Federal States of Europe, diluted with juice from fruit grown in the only orchard remaining in England, where the trees had to be pollinated by artificial bees. The pale blue liquid fizzed in the old-fashioned glass that he preferred, and was topped by a precious cherry, bought at tremendous cost from the confectioner on their recent weekend break on the Kentish coast. "You look stunning, as usual," he whispered into her ear as they embraced, and he stepped back to take in her feminine shape almost hidden beneath the folds of the metallic fabric of her dress.

"I have put out your zinc suit and silk shirt for tonight, darling."

"Must I?" he responded.

"I know you would rather wear those old jeans and a sweater, but they make you look like a leftover from the early 21st century, or one of those weird eccentrics who refuse to join the 22nd century and insist on living on one of the uninhabitable islands in the north, keeping hens and cows and horses. It's important tonight that we fit in with our fellow scientists with modern, dynamic views."

"How can I refuse such a beautiful woman anything?" murmured Richard, nuzzling her neck.

"You are sometimes so old-fashioned Sweetie, but I do like it," said Maggie. "I have ordered Rob to run you a bath, I know you like to immerse yourself in warm water." Their small servant glided into the room and his robotic tones announced that the bath was ready.

Richard took his drink with him, and sank into the luxurious bath. As he lay in the warm, sweet-smelling water, with the jets massaging his body, he drifted into a soporific state, allowing his mind to wander. He thought of his first love all those years ago. They had married very young, both in their early twenties. Two children had followed but he had abandoned his family when he fell in love with his colleague, Anna. He regretted having been such a bad father, but the times when he wanted to get in touch with them he had resisted, rather than have to explain to them why they had such a youthful father. He knew they were long gone now, and he supposed he may now have great, great, great, great-grandchildren somewhere on the planet. It seemed incredible, but true. He had never tried to find out; how could he explain this to anyone? In order to possess a believable birth certificate so he could obtain the various documents needed for modern life he had been forced to change his name several times in order to maintain the subterfuge, using the ruse described in the book written almost two hundred years ago, by Frederick Forsyth, *"The Day of the Jackal"*. By now, four identities later, he had almost forgotten Saul Anderson, that person he had once been.

"Are you still alive in there, darling?" came the voice from the bedroom. "Come along, we have to leave in half an hour."

Maggie wandered in, sitting on the end of the enormous bath.

"Julian called – they've heard from the probe. It's got as far as ISS 46, only another year to go and it should reach Excelsior."

"Well, that is going to be amazing," answered Richard as he climbed out of the bath and into the drying booth, and Maggie returned to their bedroom to finish getting ready herself.

"Do I really have to get togged up like this?" he entreated pathetically on entering the bedroom.

"You really do use the strangest expressions sometimes, Sweetie," said his puzzled partner. "I sometimes think you are a relic from another age!"

Maggie sat before the mirror, putting on her moonstone earrings, as Richard donned his silk shirt and suit, then they hailed the transporter and left for the gathering with other scientists and would-be space settlers.

The transporter covered the distance to the old town of York in 15 minutes. Richard couldn't help but think of the four hours he might once have spent on that same journey, plus an indeterminable number of hours in the event of a hold-up on one of the archaic motorways.

As they entered the fantastic building which was the home of the Interplanetary Exploration Society he noticed many familiar faces.

"Look," said Maggie, "there's Roland and Bluebell. I didn't know they had returned."

"Where was it they went to in the end?" asked Richard.

"It was Mars," answered Maggie. "They were helping to set up the staging post that is being built there."

"Hello, old chap," the voice behind Richard boomed.

"Why, Charlie. It's really good to see you," said Richard, turning to shake his old friend by the hand. "It's been too long. Are you considering applying for this trip? Maggie is really keen to go and her piloting skills are just what I think this venture needs. If she does get the post of co-pilot, I hope to be able to accompany her as the chemical analyst, with another string to my bow as part-time medic."

"I'm already part of the team," his friend replied. "Navigator through the stars."

"Well, that's very reassuring. We'll be in a safe pair of hands," said Maggie, coming to join them.

"How was Sydney?" asked Richard. He secretly found it quite incredible that for the past one hundred years hypersonic jets had been making that journey in just two hours.

"Just great," came the answer. "They have rebuilt the Harbour Bridge and although it looks very similar to the old one, it can be crossed in seconds, or you can choose to take the scenic route, which is fantastic. The old-fashioned ferries still run on the water, their trips are very popular with tourists, and you can find accommodation in the Blue Mountains, or Hunter Valley, and catch a transporter into the centre of town in ten minutes."

"How is the programme to re-introduce the Humpbacks going?" asked Maggie, who had joined them.

"Well, as you know they managed to clone some from the whale that was found five years ago in the Antarctic. The trackers on those that have been released seem to show that the creatures are confused, and not behaving as their ancestors did."

"It's criminal what we have done to the planet," said Maggie. "We have all learned a very hard lesson, and when we colonise Excelsior I know we will take more care of the environment."

"When will the announcement be made?" asked Richard. "Have you heard anything, Charlie?"

"I was asked to rate the applicants, but I've not heard the final decision. Don't worry, old boy, I gave you and Maggie a top rating. Ah! Here comes our pilot, let me introduce you. Saul, these are my old friends, Richard Martin and Maggie Francis, meet our pilot, Saul Anderson."

With a sharp intake of breath, Richard quickly regained control and held out his hand.

"Pleased to meet you. Your name sounds vaguely familiar to me," he managed to say.

"It's a family name, given to the eldest son down the generations," Saul replied.

Charlie interrupted. "Here come the announcements," and all eyes turned to the screen on the wall as the Head of the Interplanetary Exploration Society Programme came into view...

A Question of Identity

By

Pam Corsie

Pauline worked in her family's garage. She was based in the office, booking in popping exhausts, dodgy brakes and MOT tests, but often helped her dad or her brothers with the repair work, if they needed an extra pair of hands. It played havoc with her nails, although a tub of Swarfega, hot soapy water and industrial strength hand cream soon got things back on track. The men teased her constantly about her musical ambitions. She wasn't always sure just how much of it was teasing and sometimes felt hurt by their jibing. But, the show must go on, and she smiled bravely and swept any bad feeling away.

For as long as she could remember, Pauline had wanted to be a diva. She thought she was probably born too late as the sort of diva Pauline wanted to be had had her hey-day in the 1950s and 60s. Then, one evening, in the bar of the local, recently restored, art-deco theatre she had been approached by the town's self-appointed impresario, who offered her the chance to realise her dreams.

"Come and see me in the morning," he had commanded, puffing out his pigeon chest. "Ten o'clock, and don't be late. Come as you are, don't dress up."

"Yes, Mr Constantinos. Thank you, sir. I'll be there."

And she was. As the box office clock struck ten, a nervous Pauline entered the foyer to be confronted by all 5 foot 3 of Mr Constantinos, striding up and down the marble floor on his little legs, shouting into his mobile. She hadn't dressed up, but had applied her make-up carefully and was wearing her best dress and matching red heels.

"Come on," he said, stuffing his mobile into his jacket and making a grab for Pauline's hand. He dragged her into his office and said, "I've heard about you from the landlord of the White Hart. He says you're a regular at their karaoke nights. Bring the house down, you do, with your Shirley Bassey. He reckons you'd be a draw for the Revue here at the Grand. D'ya reckon you could pull in the punters?"

"Oh yes, Mr Constantinos. I'm sure I could. I'd certainly give it a good try."

"Good tries aren't good enough. Rehearsals start at ten thirty this morning. I'll tell you if you're good enough to be in the show or not. No costumes, just you. I need to make sure that you can sing as well as look the part."

"Yes, Mr Constantinos. Point me in the right direction, please, and I'll blow your socks off."

"That's the ticket, love." Shoving her out of the door, he added, "The stage manager and the other acts should be there by now. I'm taking a big chance on you. Don't let me down."

"Yes, Mr Constantinos, no, Mr Constantinos."

The walls and ceiling of the auditorium were ornate, decorated with ceiling roses, frescoes and a mural on one wall, depicting everyone who had helped with the cost of the refurbishment. If Pauline looked closely she could see herself, three rows from the bottom of the painting, smiling wistfully at the stage. Not a very flattering portrait, she'd thought, originally, but she had become accustomed to the way she looked in the mural and, although still not delighted by it, had come to accept the face assigned to her.

She walked down the aisle, between the newly upholstered, red, plush seats, to the stage. "Pauline," boomed a voice from the third row, "I believe you're our Shirley, love."

"I hope so, sir," she replied and almost bobbed a curtsey.

"No need for that, Shirley. We're all equal here, each as good as our last performance. Now, let's see what you're made of."

He ruled with a rod of iron, but was really a kindly man who looked after everyone's welfare with avuncular charm that got the best out of all the performers. Pauline was instantly won over by his large personality and fair approach and her butterflies retreated. Her big chance! She belted out *Goldfinger*, *Big Spender* and *Diamonds Are Forever*. The rest of the cast applauded and cheered loudly when she had finished. Pauline stood proud and smiling, thrilled to bits with herself.

Mr Constantinos walked from where he had been standing in the shadows, clapping his hands and grinning. He gave a surreptitious nod in the direction of the Stage Manager and an ecstatic Pauline was in.

That was yesterday. Mr Constantinos didn't waste any time.

"Start tomorrow night," he said, "first on, after the intermission, and we'll see how you're received before we decide on your place on the bill."

The skittering butterflies were back. Pauline had hardly eaten since yesterday. She had told her family about her successful audition and had received mixed reactions. Her brothers and mum wanted to know if they could get tickets but dad didn't look quite so keen. Mum would soon talk him round.

She was so nervous. Her throat was as dry as the Sahara, but, like the trooper she impersonated, she gulped back a warm, honey concoction, slathered on pan stick, applied false eyelashes and painted her lips red. She shimmied gracefully into the silver evening dress, ran her hands over her hips, stepped into the rhinestone-covered, silver heels and smoothed her glossy, beehive wig.

"Yes!" she whispered to herself. "This is it!"

"Five minutes, Miss Bassey," someone called and tapped on the dressing room door. She picked up her sequined microphone with a bejewelled, manicured hand and started her journey to the stage.

Fifty steps max, Pauline thought, swallowing hard. That's all and it feels like a million miles and a new life. As she smiled to herself, she spotted her family in the wings. The show was a sell-out but Mr Constantinos had come up trumps and invited her family to watch from backstage, saying this could be the start of something big and they should be there, dad included.

As the band played the opening notes of *I Am What I Am*, Pauline took a deep breath, slapped on a smile and stepped into the spotlight. Paul was looking forward to ditching his alter-ego, Pauline. Shirley Bassey was such a huge step up. He'd waited a long time for this moment.

Canteen Curry

By

Shelagh O'Grady

I awake to find sunlight streaming through the window and a loud knocking on the door. A man's voice shouts "Rise and shine, lazy bones! We've got a briefing in half an hour."

My brain, still fuzzy from sleep, is trying to recall where I am. Crawling from under the scratchy bed covers I look around but don't recognise the room. I am sitting on an iron bedstead with a thin mattress and coarse-looking bedcovers. Looking around, the room appears to be prefabricated, painted a pale green colour and in need of a good clean. Draped over an old-fashioned straight-backed chair hang my clothes, well, not my clothes but they are the only ones I can see. Standing up, I realise that my T-shirt and boxers have now become blue and white striped pyjamas.

Shaking my head and rubbing my eyes I try to bring myself back to reality as I inspect the clothes on the chair. Recoiling in horror I recognise the blue/grey coloured outfit to be flying gear of the Second World War. Pacing to the window I look out onto a large expanse of grass with tarmac strips running away into the distance.

"Get a move on Tim, you'll miss your breakfast, mate," comes the voice again followed by another thumping on the door. I dress quickly in the clothes on the chair, my brain unable to process logical thought, and then check myself in the grimy mirror.

"My God!" I cry, as I stare at the reflection. Instead of a bearded, fair-haired 38-year-old I see a dark-haired handsome youth of maybe 20 years with eyes that have witnessed horror and destruction far beyond their tender years. In a state of shock I head for the door, pull it open and stumble into a corridor.

"Up at last! Come on mate, you've just got time for a mug of tea and bacon butty if you hurry."

"Thanks," I mutter as I follow a similarly dressed young man into a canteen.

"You look shattered, Tim. Are you ok? I know we had a few beers last night but you can usually handle that. Here, drink your tea, it'll clear your head."

"Thanks," I say again as he pushes an enamel mug filled with hot, strong-looking tea into my hands. "I feel quite disorientated, as if I'm another person," I add.

"Maybe it was last night's dinner. That canteen curry can do awful things to you. Here, try a bacon butty. That should settle you down."

"Yeah, maybe," I reply as I bite into the thick, greyish looking bread.

Glancing around the canteen I find it full of young men dressed like me, in flying gear. Am I really in the Second World War, at some airfield, ready to take off in a plane and fight the Germans? Whatever happened last night? I'm supposed to be on my way to a conference in New York representing the company at an international convention. If this is a dream it feels very real. How do I wake up and get back to reality?

My mate, I learn his name is Bob, shepherds me and a few others into a room full of chairs set in rows facing a blackboard covered with diagrams. The station commander stands before us detailing the raid we will be flying tonight, a bombing run on a group of German factories and power plants.

I listen in stunned silence. A calendar on the wall tells me it is October 1942. It seems as if I am taking part in an epic war film but the set appears too realistic. I feel myself being drawn into it all, the present overpowering my past life and who I was. Whatever happened last night must have been something quite powerful, and now it holds me too tightly to escape. I decide I must now play along and hope for some kind of release.

After lunch and a kick around with an old-fashioned leather football I find myself playing cards with several members of the group. My card skills are quite good, better than I remember them.

As the chilly autumn evening draws in we receive our flying orders and will be taking off at 1800 hours. There is a feeling of apprehension, the tension experienced before each flying mission. The bustle of men has a purpose and Bob suggests I get my gear ready.

"OK," I reply and head back to my room. "What gear am I supposed to have?" I ask myself. I open the wardrobe and find heavy boots, a fur-lined flying jacket and a helmet, all of which I put on. The situation is getting quite serious now. If this is some kind of film set it's frighteningly real. I rejoin the group and we walk out into the gathering gloom.

"Are you OK now?" asks Bob as he walks beside me. "Your head seemed a bit muddled this morning. I need you to be thinking clearly on this mission tonight."

"I'm fine now, thanks. It probably was that curry," I reply, picking up on the excuse previously volunteered. "I'll be OK when we get airborne." What made me say that, I wonder?

As we walk across the tarmac I can make out the shape of a huge plane which I recognise as a Lancaster bomber. This is too real for a film set and now I feel panic churning in the pit of my stomach. I climb aboard and sit with some other guys on seats inside the fuselage. We strap ourselves in and Bob takes his place in the pilot's seat.

As the engines start the noise is deafening. I sit in the dark, hanging onto my seat and praying I will wake up soon. As the huge plane moves down the runway I feel the G-forces pulling my body into the seat. The motion changes as we lift into the air, this huge metal bird with me strapped inside takes off into the night sky heading towards Germany and whatever awaits us.

My palms are sweaty, my breathing shallow and there's a heavy lump in my stomach. I have never felt so afraid. We seem to fly for hours and I am feeling very cold. Eventually Bob's voice, crackling with static, comes over the intercom.

"Approaching target area, take your stations before we descend. Watch out everyone, there's a lot of flak below us. I'm relying on you Tim, my trusty rear gunner, to keep the Hun off our tail. Good luck everyone!"

Rear gunner! Oh hell!

I unbuckle and make my way to the rear of the plane. Oddly enough I seem to know the way. I squeeze into my seat behind the huge gun and automatically begin my checks. The gun is already loaded and the ammunition belts are stacked up beside me. As I touch the cold metal I feel a sense of familiarity with it all and I know what to do. I try not to think how I know but just follow what has to be.

We fly into the target area and I am shooting at enemy planes as they approach. I sense I have done this many times before and feel quite confident. One plane falls away and explodes in a ball of fire and I call out my hit.

"Your hit noted," crackles back over the intercom.

"Bombs away," says a different voice.

"OK, let's get out of here," Bob's voice calls through the static.

Suddenly there is a huge explosion in the plane and fire is racing through the fuselage. We have been hit. I start to release my harness but as the flames reach me I lose consciousness.

I awake with a bright light shining overhead. People are looking at me and I can't move.

"Hello Tim, can you hear me?" asks a pretty nurse standing in my line of vision. I try to speak but my mouth is dry so I nod slightly and stare at her. She is wearing a modern-day uniform and the equipment around is definitely twenty-first century.

"I'm back," I think to myself, hardly daring to believe it. "But what the hell happened?"

The nurse helps me with a sip of water and I croak "What year is it?"

A puzzled expression crosses her face. "2017," she says.

"Thank God!" I reply. Then I realise that she has an American accent. "What happened? Where am I?"

"You are in a New York hospital. Your flight from London to New York suffered a terrorist attack. A small device caused an explosion and blew a hole in the fuselage. Luckily the plane was preparing to land and was fairly low over the sea when it happened. Your seat was near the back and the tail section remained intact on landing. You were pulled from the sea three days ago."

I feel stunned; I can't describe the emotions spinning around in my head.

"Is it really 2017?" I ask again.

"It sure is, and it's a fine October day."

The Gift

By

Pam Sawyer

"She's had it lads, we are going to bail out," Eddie shouted above the noise of the engine. He had seen the fire on one of the starboard engines and the cockpit was filling with fumes. He knew he would not have control of the plane for very much longer. The bombing raid had been successful but as they turned for home they were hit by anti-aircraft fire.

The crew strapped on their parachutes. Reg, the rear gunner, called out, "Eddie, Jonno won't be coming with us." Reg had found Jonno the navigator slumped forward, covered in blood.

"Righto chaps, it's now or never." The remaining crewmembers jumped one by one, Eddie being the last to leave the stricken aeroplane.

"Bye old girl, do as much damage as you can, try and land on Gerry." The plane flew on, rapidly losing height before crashing into a wood, the surrounding area lit up by the explosion and flames. Eddie and Reg landed close together and quickly took off their parachutes, they stuffed them in a hedge, not the best hiding place but hopefully they would stay hidden while the men got away. They knew they had to get as far as possible from the aeroplane as the crash would have alerted the Germans.

It was a starlit night with no moon. As far as they were aware they were somewhere in Northern France. The main object being to stay clear of the enemy, Eddie and Reg gave low whistles to attract the attention of the others. They waited but there was no answering whistle.

"Just you and me then Reg." They made their way across a field moving quickly not talking. They reached a narrow road and set off at a brisk walk, their eyes now accustomed to the dark.

"What's the plan then, Eddie?"

"Haven't got one yet, I'll probably make it up as we go along. Reg, do you speak French?"

"Nah, never saw the need, well not down the east end, not many froggies there. Why, do you?"

"A bit, came here on holiday a few times back in the twenties."

They had been walking for an hour and dawn was beginning to break. They would soon need to hide, as it got lighter. As the sun rose they now knew which direction they should be heading. They had been walking north which was their first bit of luck, and although it was the end of October the sun felt quite warm.

"God, I'm starving, I could eat an 'orse." Reg settled himself down in the small copse they had managed to hide in.

"Yep, food is our next priority, but let's try and get a bit of shuteye." Eddie was worried that they were a bit too close to the road.

Presently they heard the sound of a car coming down the road. Cautiously looking out Eddie saw an old Citroen, a young woman at the wheel. At the same time coming in the other direction was a German soldier on a motorcycle. He signalled for the woman to stop, and slowly dismounting he went over to the car. Opening the driver's door he motioned for her to get out.

"Papers." he snarled. The woman, her hands shaking, took her papers from her handbag. Eddie crawled a bit closer to the road as the soldier looked over the papers. She was quite young and pretty with dark, curly hair. She looked terrified.

"Ah, Jew," he smirked. Opening the back door to the car he leaned in and, grabbing what looked like a hold-all, he opened it up. Eddie and Reg were amazed to hear a baby cry. The woman made a grab for the bag and the soldier threw it down. He caught hold of the woman and as he pushed her into the back of the car, he snatched at a gold chain round her neck. Eddie was horrified to see him undo his trouser belt and braces. Christ, he thought, he's going to rape her.

He carefully drew his RAF issue .45 Colt pistol from its holster, creeping forward. The woman was screaming as Eddie leapt from behind the car and fired at the soldier. Blood spurted from his neck as he sank to the ground clutching his throat, a look of surprise on his face. Reg had now come out of his hiding place.

"See to the woman, I'll deal with the bike." Eddie went over to the motorcycle and pushed it away into the copse. Looking around, he now had to deal with the dead soldier. He grabbed the body under the arms. "Come on, Fritz, time for you to go hidey hidey." He dragged it into the copse next to the motorcycle. Searching through the soldier's uniform he took a Luger pistol from its holster. "You won't be needing that, old chum."

Reg put his arm round the woman, who was shaking.

"My baby, my baby." Eddie picked up the child. He stuck his finger in its mouth and it stopped crying immediately. The woman calmed down and Eddie gave her back the baby.

"Thank you, thank you." Looking at them, she said, "The aeroplane last night? You?"

Eddie nodded. "It is too dangerous for you to be on this road. There are a lot of Germans hereabouts."

She opened the car door and said, "Come with me, I can take you somewhere for help." Reg and Eddie got in the car, Reg in the back with the baby and Eddie in the front.

"Hey Eddie, what was that trick with the baby and your finger?"

"My parents have a farm and it works with calves when they have to be weaned and separated from their mothers."

"Well I'll be … you're a dark horse and no mistake."

As they drove, Eddie complimented the woman, Marthe as she asked him to call her, on her English. She told him she was a schoolteacher but had lost her job last year as she was Jewish. Her husband, his brother and their uncle had all been arrested and she hadn't heard or seen anything of them for six months. Soon the woman turned off the road and up a long track to a farmhouse.

"You will be safe here, they will give you clothes and arrange for you to be moved further on towards the coast."

"Where will you go?" Eddie asked Marthe.

"I have friends in the next village, I am staying there. Tell me Eddie, do you have a wife?"

"No, not yet."

"A sweetheart maybe?"

"Yes, and I hope once this damn war is over she will be my wife."

"Please give her this." She pulled the gold chain from her neck; it had a small, gold Star of David and an amethyst and diamond pendant.

"I can't take that, it must be very valuable."

"Not as valuable as his or my life." She pointed to the baby.

"That pig would have killed us both after …" Her voice trailed off. "Please take it, give it to your sweetheart."

Reluctantly Eddie took the pendant but removed the Star of David. "You should keep this."

Taking it, she said, "Eddie and Reg, I cannot thank you enough for saving us, I wish you both much luck and I hope, Eddie, you get back to your sweetheart soon, and now we must go and meet Jean-Paul and Marie-Thérèse, his wife. They will take good care of you, especially when I tell them of your brave actions this morning."

Eddie and Reg, Marthe and her baby went into the farmhouse.

On The Road

By

Angie Simpkins

"Are we there yet?" came the plaintiff cry from the back seat.

"Do stop asking that every five minutes," said Julie, George's exasperated mother, as she looked ahead and saw a sudden explosion of red brake lights.

"Don't like the look of this," muttered Mike under his breath in order not to be heard in the back of the car, and they travelled just a couple of hundred yards more before finally coming to a halt.

"Mum, look at that man in the white van, he's on the phone, I thought that was illegal. Shall we report him?" said George. "And look at that red and green lorry, the wheels are enormous."

Mike sat there drumming his fingers on the steering wheel, and Julie rummaged in the bag at her feet and found a bag of sweets which she passed round.

"Mum, he's taken my favourite pink one," screeched Amelia as she tried to wrestle the pink delight from her brother, who eventually succeeded in getting the fruit chew into his mouth, and screwed his eyes up in ecstasy, saying "scrumptious."

They sat quietly for five minutes, unable to move forward, when they heard the sound of approaching sirens. First a police car with blue lights flashing and siren screeching passed at speed on the hard shoulder, shortly followed by a fire engine, then an ambulance. George undid his seat belt and leapt up excitedly, watching the emergency vehicles as they sped away.

"George, sit down and do up your seat belt," said his father, crossly.

"Look, Dad, people are getting out of their cars and walking about," said George, "Can't we get out too?"

Just then a face peered in at the driver's window.

"Right palaver this is, isn't it mate?" said the burly man as he lit a roll-up. "I'm supposed to be in Nottingham at 3 o'clock, doesn't look like I'll make it. Don't suppose you've got a phone I could use – my battery's run out."

"Hand me your phone, Julie," said Mike as he unbuckled his seat belt and opened the door of the car. "Here you are," he said, handing the phone over. "Might as well stretch my legs."

"Mum, Mum, can't we get out too?" cried George. "Oh well, I suppose so, but you must stay close to me," said Julie, and they all climbed out of the car.

She looked around her. There was a man walking two big dogs along the grass verge bordering the hard shoulder, and a small child being helped to wee on the same grass verge, and many people standing by their cars chatting to other motorists. They climbed to the top of the bank, it was surreal she thought, when normally we just speed by, with no time to study the beautiful flowers on the grassy bank, which was alight with cowslips, or to look at the quintessentially English view from the top of the bank, from which she could see the peaceful meadows and on the far bank of a small river a typical village scene with a church spire reaching up into the sky.

As she looked down on the scene below with the lines of stationary traffic stretching ahead and behind, she noticed two men in uniform and high-vis jackets walking among the vehicles.

"We'd better get back to the car," she told the children, and they clambered down the slippery bank just in time to see Mike talking to one of the policemen.

"There's been an accident up ahead. We're working on clearing the road but it's likely to take another hour or so," was the message that the policeman was giving to the stranded motorists.

"Look, Mum, look at his handcuffs!" said an excited George

"Well, sonny, you seem to be enjoying today, even if no-one else is," said the avuncular policeman, moving on along the lines of traffic, with a parting shot of "keep off the hard shoulder" just as another ambulance came speeding along, siren blaring and blue lights flashing.

"I want to be a policeman when I grow up," said George, and "I want to drive an ambulance," said Amelia, having noticed the blonde ponytail worn by the ambulance driver as she sped by.

As Julie turned to look at her daughter, an extremely agitated young man got out of the old Ford Fiesta in front of them and ran up to Julie.

"My wife's in labour, she's having a baby and I don't know what to do," he stammered.

"Oh, my goodness," thought Julie. "Mike, go and find one of the policemen, tell them there's a woman in labour here and get some help. You children, get back in the car immediately. Amelia, the sweets are in my bag, you can both have another," and she followed the panic-stricken young man to his car where she found a pretty young woman in obvious distress.

"My waters have broken," she told Julie.

"Well, try not to worry too much," Julie replied. "That doesn't necessarily mean that the birth is imminent. My husband has gone to get help. What is your name?"

"Emily," came the reply.

"My name is Julie," said Julie as she climbed into the front seat next to Emily, and took her hand, "and I do know a little about having a baby, having had two of my own. Are you having contractions?"

"I don't think so," replied Emily.

"Well, that means we've plenty of time," said Julie in an attempt to reassure the young woman, at the same time making a valiant attempt at not showing her own feelings of helplessness. "Mike, my husband, has gone to get one of the policemen. I'm sure they will know what to do, and they can call for an ambulance. we've already seen two speeding along the hard shoulder, so there should be no problem in getting one for you."

"I wanted my Mum to be here when the baby comes," cried Emily.

"I'm here Bunnykins," came a voice from the back seat. "Don't cry. We'll phone her as soon as there's any news. She can't wait to meet her first grandchild," he explained to Julie.

"It's a very exciting time for you all, I remember it well. Do you know if it's to be a boy or a girl?" asked Julie.

"No, we decided we didn't want to know beforehand," said Emily, who seemed to have calmed down a little. Just then Mike returned with the same policeman who had spoken to them earlier.

"Now then, what have we here?" said the jolly voice as his large face appeared at the car window. "Don't you worry my duck, it won't be the first babe I've brought into the world, although I'd rather not do it on the M1 – what a place to put on the birth certificate! I've radioed for an ambulance, and the paramedics will be here soon. If you weren't all drivers, I would say this calls for Champagne to wet the baby's head."

Emily's husband, Paul, fought back tears of relief as he realised that he was surrounded by people who would know what to do and could take care of Emily and their little one. "Thank you all so much," he mumbled.

They sat in the car for what seemed ages. PC Hancock waited outside and wandered up and down, not moving far away. Mike returned to his own car where the children were avid for information as to what was going on. Mike explained the situation to them, which only increased their excitement.

"Dad, can we get out again?" whined Amelia. "I really want to see the ambulance when it arrives."

"Alright," said their father, "but you must stay close to me."

On hearing the wailing ambulance, PC Hancock went to the hard shoulder and held up his hand. The ambulance halted and the driver and accompanying paramedic, carrying a large bag, got out. Amelia gazed in awe at the two women in green uniforms who made their way confidently, following PC Hancock, to the old Ford car. Julie climbed out and one of the paramedics got in her place, the other slid in the back next to Paul. Amelia watched in admiration as they spoke to Emily and put a cuff on her arm.

"What are they doing, Mum?" she asked.

"Taking her blood pressure," was the reply. Then the quartet got out of the car, and with Emily supported on one side by Paul, and the other by a paramedic, they all got into the back of the ambulance, and closed the door.

"What's happening now?" Amelia wanted to know, thoroughly relishing what she perceived as a drama happening right in front of her eyes.

"Well," said Julie. "Emily has got good care, we might as well have our picnic lunch here as it looks as if we are going to be here for some time. We could climb to the top of the embankment and sit there, and keep an eye on the situation from that lofty viewpoint."

So, getting the bags from the boot of the car, they all climbed to the top of the bank and spread out the food.

"I must say, this is the first time I've had a picnic on the M1 waiting for the birth of a baby," said Mike, munching on a sausage roll. "It seems really weird. It's not what I envisaged when we left home this morning, but there could be worse places I suppose."

"We could be up ahead in the cars that all these emergency vehicles have been racing to," said Julie. "I for one am just grateful that it's not us."

The children began exploring their eyrie, and George found a good tree to climb. Julie and Mike sat back and tried to enjoy the sunshine.

"I wonder what time we'll arrive at the hotel," thought Mike aloud. "If we don't get moving soon, I'll have to phone to explain the delay."

Before Julie could reply, the doors of the ambulance were flung open, and an ecstatic Paul emerged, looking round and shouting "It's a boy, it's a boy!"

Julie scrambled down the bank as fast as she could, and on seeing her Paul threw his arms around her. "Come and see, come and see!" he cried.

Julie stepped gingerly into the ambulance, to see a smiling Emily nursing a red-faced little bundle. "Thank you so much," she said. I'll never forget you, or today."

"I don't think any of us will," said Julie beaming.

Double Trouble

By

Pam Corsie

It was that time of year again – Halloween – when the greedy, ghastly children of the neighbourhood came knocking on the door. They were always dressed in shop-bought costumes, clutching empty bags to be filled with sweets by supposedly terrified householders, who had been idiotic enough to answer the ring on the door bell. The cry of "Trick or Treat" would echo all evening long in the eerie streets.

Evelyn pulled her thin cardigan around her scrawny shoulders and crouched over the measly fire in the grate in the back room. She looked around at the dusty curtains, grubby windows, faded wallpaper, balding, velvet tablecloth and general decay. It's no longer wear and tear, she thought. It's been years since Mother went and I haven't changed a thing. I still feel her presence when I sit here, in her seat, in front of this sad, spluttering fire. Her recall of Mother's words had not faded over time.

"Evelyn, move away from the fire. Fetch me my book of spells and that big dish. I'll soon mix up something for you. Never fear, I'll find you a man, somehow or other." Bending low over the mixing bowl, Mother muttered and cursed quietly, all the while stirring the concoction on her lap with the wooden spoon held in her gnarled hands. "Here, drink this, you will be beautiful before you know it."

Evelyn had started off thinking she was reasonably attractive, almost pretty, but mother had soon put that idea out of her head. "Look at that rats-tail hair, those stringy arms and shapeless body. How are you ever going to get a man?" Mother ranted.

Evelyn thought she bore more than a passing resemblance to her mother. Presumably, Mother must have found herself a man somewhere or else there wouldn't have been an Evelyn.

She rolled the dice backward and forward between her two hands. Even number totals meant she could do something, odd meant she had to stay in the chair. She tossed them onto the rickety table she sat beside – a three and a one. As she rose from the seat, she noticed the night had begun to draw in and Evelyn carefully pulled the tatty curtains together across the grimy window. She returned to the chair and threw a four and a six. She carefully placed a spindly log, more of a stick really, on the fire.

She mulled disdainfully over the idea of a shop-bought Halloween costume. Mother always said she should make her own as it was much more fun. It had been quite good fun sometimes, the more tomato ketchup smeared on the ghostly sheet, the better, as far as Evelyn was concerned. The more people that recoiled in horror gave her a greater sense of power and then Mother had been so proud of her. On reflection though, Evelyn had to admit that it was difficult to make the excitement of one night last all year, until Mother became engaged again.

Evelyn felt a cold draught across her shoulders, through the worn, unravelling cardigan. "Hello, Mum," she whispered. "I wondered if I would be seeing you tonight."

"My favourite night of the year, Evelyn. Always was, and always will be, especially now that no-one can see me coming, if I don't want them to. Have you bought the goodies for the little horrors when they come tolling on the door bell, shouting and yelling?"

"Yes, Mother, they are in a tin by the front door. Mum," she whispered. "I hope you are going to behave this year. You will be gentle with the children won't you? I got into a terrible mess last year, after you'd gone. Eggs, flour, all sorts of rubbish thrown at the house. The cat was petrified."

"That cat should be petrified. I never understood why it didn't come with me when I went to the other side."

"Maybe it likes real life. Maybe it likes me!"

"Huh, don't be ridiculous. Who would prefer you to me? Was that the doorbell? Is this the first of the little monsters?"

Evelyn threw the dice again onto the table, the cat shrieked and leapt out from his hiding place beneath it, making a sharp left into the hall to avoid Mother's grasping, claw-like hands. It was a double three. Evelyn sighed heavily – doubles meant that mother got to choose the action.

"Ha ha," Mother cackled. "Come on, shake yourself, you answer the door."

Evelyn walked slowly along the moth-eaten hall runner towards the front door.

"Come on, girl, move yourself, they'll be gone before you get there and we'll have no fun at all."

As she approached the front door, Evelyn wished her hardest that Mother would vanish as she sometimes did, for no reason. She wished in vain, there was no chance of that tonight – Halloween was a very special time for Mother.

The obedient daughter slowly released the bolt and turned the handle on the front door.

"Trick or treat!" screeched six small children. They were dressed as vampires, ghosts, ghouls and, weirdly, a princess and bounced up and down in the porch whilst thrusting specially designed goody bags up at her.

"Treat, I think," said Evelyn warily, as she held out a tin of sweets. Six grasping hands fought their way into the tin, plunging and rummaging, each trying to pick up as many sweets as they could with one grab, knowing that a second grab wasn't allowed. They turned, without saying thank you, and ran off.

"She could be a witch." Evelyn heard one little boy say as he skipped back down the overgrown path.

The gust of cold wind made Evelyn jump as it whooshed passed her, down the path and whipped the little boy's cheap, tacky costume over his head. He tripped over a loose paving stone and one of the girls screamed and another yelled, "She's put a spell on you and made you fall over."

Evelyn slammed the door quickly. "Mother! How could you? I don't suppose he's more than eight years old."

"Well, if he wants to make nine, he'd better mind his manners."

Mother strode authoritatively, and Evelyn crept, back to the dreary room at the rear of the house. The door bell sounded again. "Another lamb to the slaughter, it's like Waterloo station here tonight," cackled Mother, rubbing her hands together.

The dice added up to a total of five this time. Evelyn did not know what was worse, Mother telling her what to do, or Mother answering the door herself as the odd number ordered. She leapt to her feet and followed the cloud of dust and stale perfume that surrounded her mother to the front door. Mother flung the door back on its hinges, "Trick or trea..." The words died on the lips of the tall child at the front of the group. He turned a deathly shade of pale and his group of tiny followers screamed and clutched their goody bags close to their chests. All except for one, a stout little chap of five or six, who stepped forward and grabbed a handful of Mother's ragged garment.

"You must be in there somewhere," he yelled. "I want my treat." His friends each took a step back, treading on each other in their haste to retreat and a couple of them fell to the floor. The tubby lad bravely yanked on the dusty robes. They reared up with an unearthly wail and threw themselves across the two prostrate children on the path.

"Help, help, aaah, oh no, save us!" was the combined cry of the children. Their 'courageous' parents were calling them to come back to sanctuary behind the garden wall where they waited and watched, too scared to venture forward and help their offspring. The pile of dusty rags rose up with a blood curdling cackle allowing the two terrified children to scramble out from beneath and race for the broken gate at the end of the path.

Scared parents, trying to be brave, gathered their children to them, uttering soothing words whilst looking over their shoulders at the screeching, floating, swirling rags retreating to the inside of the house.

Mother materialised from inside the dusty rags when the front door was safely shut. She was caterwauling with laughter as she tried to tell Evelyn how funny it all was, how scared the children were, and how pathetic were their parents. "I know, Mother, I heard it all and saw most of it. Why do you do this to me? I have to live here the rest of the year. I can't go swanning off like you do, to wherever you decide to go."

"Why ever not?"

"I have to stay here. One day, a handsome young man may come for me and I don't want to miss him. And, anyway, I have to feed the cat."

Evelyn scuffed her way to the back room. Mother, two paces behind her, prodding her in the back, giving a squawking rendition of "*Someday My Prince Will Come*," followed on and they eventually sat down either side of the dismal fire. They had barely got comfortable and, thankfully, Mother did not have the chance to finish her song, when the doorbell rang again.

Evelyn threw the dice – double six. Oh no, Mother's won again. "Open the door slow coach," Mother ordered, grinning gleefully.

Evelyn sidled slowly along the hall and gingerly opened the front door. "Trick or treat?" came a gruff voice from within the costume of a man carrying his own head under his arm. This trick or treater was alone and appeared far too old to be out begging for sweets.

"Treat, I think," Evelyn heard herself say. "Perhaps you'd like to come in for something to warm you, on this cold night?"

"Don't mind if I do," the gruff voice replied, and Evelyn felt the cold wind blast him towards the back of the house as he shot past her and purposefully walked down the hall.

She followed him nervously and said, "Sit yourself by the fire and I'll fix you a nice hot toddy. I'm Evelyn, by the way," she introduced herself, "and you are?"

"James, James Prince," said the gruff voice. "Do you mind if I put my head on the table? It's awfully heavy." He swivelled towards the table which rocked precariously on its uneven legs and put his head on the velvet cloth.

"Of, of, of course not," Evelyn stammered. "Take off your cloak too, or the heat from that paltry fire will take a long time to get through to your bones."

"Thanks, but I don't really feel the cold anymore."

Evelyn didn't catch all that he said as she dashed into the kitchen where Mother was waiting. The ingredients for a steaming hot toddy were simmering in a bowl on the old stove. Two large pewter goblets were placed, waiting expectantly, on a nearby shelf.

"Now Evelyn, you're doing really well. You've got him inside, now give him this love potion and soon he will be eating out of your hand."

Evelyn threw the dice, double two. She must obey her mother. It usually made things easier to obey Mother, rather than argue and then end up having to make decisions for herself. So she poured two steaming helpings of her mother's potion into the goblets and made her way into the back room and the poor, unsuspecting James Prince.

"Here you are," she said, holding out one of the goblets as she entered the room, "this should soon get you warm again. I'll have one too, this fire is just not good enough for the job."

"I'm not sure if I'll ever be warm again," cackled the head on the table. James, the headless man sitting next to it, poured the whole contents of the goblet into the open mouth.

"Delicious," the head cried and winked at Evelyn.

"Oh Mother, what have you done now?"

Raindrop Racing

By

Shelagh O'Grady

Paul sat miserably beside the window gazing at the rain. He longed to ride his new bike. Idly he watched the raindrops running down the window, starting at the top and sliding downwards, bumping into others as they went. They seemed to be having such fun! Suddenly Paul heard a voice calling his name but when he looked round he couldn't see anyone.

"Where are you?" he asked.

"I'm here, I'm a raindrop sliding down the window," came the reply. Paul looked in amazement.

"Come and play with us," called the voice.

"How do I do that?" he asked.

"Easy. Press your nose with your finger and wish yourself up here," laughed the raindrop. Paul placed his finger onto his nose and pressed gently whilst he wished that he could join the raindrops. Immediately he became very small and found himself standing on a ledge at the top of the window.

"Come on!" called a big raindrop, "Sit on me and hold tight!"

Paul did as he was told and the raindrop set off down the window pane, sliding past other raindrops clinging to the glass. Ahead was a large raindrop which had stopped.

Oh dear, we're going to crash! thought Paul. He shut his eyes and waited for the bump. It was like crashing into a balloon. He opened his eyes and saw the other raindrop sliding down beside them.

"Did that frighten you?" it asked.

"Just a bit," replied Paul.

"We're always bumping into each other, it's great fun!" came the cheery reply.

Paul was starting to enjoy this game and he smiled happily. The raindrops continued to slide down the window, laughing and bumping into each other. Soon a large group were sliding down with Paul in the middle.

"Whee!" he shouted. "This is great!"

Suddenly, Paul saw the window sill just beneath them and they were heading straight for it!

"Oh dear, how do we stop?" he gasped, starting to feel frightened. The window sill was approaching very fast and Paul couldn't bear to look. He shut his eyes tight and waited for the awful bump. Instead there was a big splash and Paul felt himself floating. Slowly he opened his eyes and found that he was sitting astride a bubble floating towards the edge of a puddle.

"Did you enjoy the ride?" called a voice.

"It was great!" exclaimed Paul as he looked around. "But where are you?"

"I'm part of the puddle now," came the reply.

"Won't I be able to play with you again?" asked Paul sadly.

"Don't worry, my friends are on the window waiting to play with you. I'll see you again on another rainy day," called the voice, sounding fainter.

"How do I get to the top of the window again?" asked Paul.

"Press your nose and wish. Goodbye, Paul." The voice faded away.

"Thank you, goodbye," he replied as he pressed his nose.

Almost before he could make his wish he was back at the top of the window with the other raindrops.

"Come on, Paul," they called. "Climb on and we'll race to the bottom."

Paul jumped onto a fat raindrop that wobbled like a jelly and they set off. He held on tightly and laughed as they bumped into another raindrop and went racing past others. When they arrived at the bottom they splashed into the puddle and Paul floated to the edge on a bubble. Pressing his nose he wished himself to the top of the window again. This was such fun!

Paul had just started his sixth run when he heard a familiar voice calling him. Sitting up, he was surprised to find that he was back home beside the window and Mummy was calling him.

"Paul, wake up. You've been asleep!"

"No, I haven't. I've been sliding down the window with the raindrops," giggled Paul.

"You've been dreaming!" laughed Mummy. "Look, the rain has stopped and the sky is clearing. You will soon be able to go outside and ride your bike."

Paul looked at the window and watched as one last raindrop ran down the glass and plopped into the puddle. Putting his finger to his nose he wondered if it had all been a dream. He would find out the next time it rained.

The Bunch of Flowers

By

Angie Simpkins

"There's another one," said Margaret to herself as she surveyed the small bunch of lilies of the valley laying on top of the grave. She had lost count of the number of times she had discovered a bunch of flowers laid on top of her son's grave. She could only visit on Wednesday afternoons because that was the only day of the week that the bus took the route through the village where she had grown up, and where she and Stan had brought up their three children. She had returned to Kingswood each week since that awful day three months ago when she and Stan had seen their son, Peter, laid to rest, and now it seemed as if Stan would soon be joining him.

She sat on the old bench in the churchyard and began to weep. The doctors had said that Stan's heart attack was probably caused by the shock and grief of Peter's death in Afghanistan. They had both been devastated by the news, and felt very much alone as the twins, Jennie and Mark, had both emigrated to Australia with their families. The afternoon grew chilly, and she pulled up her coat collar and reminded herself that she had to be at the bus stop in half an hour. She sat in the peaceful place and racked her brains to think who it could be who was bringing flowers to Peter's grave. How could she find out? She looked around for someone else, but the place was deserted. Eventually she got up reluctantly and made her way back to the bus stop in the village.

When she got home she told Stan about the flowers, and he was as mystified as she was. "If only I could drive again, we could visit more often and at different times, we might be able to discover something then," said Stan wistfully. "Let's see what the doctor has to say on Friday."

Friday dawned and the patient transport arrived at eight o'clock to collect Stan. Margaret busied herself with cleaning and baking while Stan was away. She knew he was unlikely to be returned until late in the afternoon. At five o'clock she heard the ambulance, and went to the door. Stan was being helped up the path by the young woman driver, but he was actually walking. "There you go, me duck," said Molly as she guided Stan over the step, "that's better than being pushed in the chair, isn't it?"

"Thanks, Molly," said Stan and Margaret in unison, and he leant on his wife as she guided him to the chair. "The doc says I am improving," Stan told Margaret, "and if I continue he thinks I might be able to drive again in a few weeks' time, I've just got to have a few more tests first."

Life continued as before, except that Stan did seem to be recovering, and eventually he returned from a hospital visit, walking unaided up the drive, excitedly declaring that he had now been given the all clear to drive. "We can get out and about a bit, see some of the countryside, and visit Kingswood again, even have lunch out," he said. Margaret had of course continued with her Wednesday afternoon visits, and there had been more flowers, but still no sign of who had left them.

The following Sunday after lunch Stan was in good spirits. "How about we go for a little drive?" he asked. "We could go to Kingswood and take Peter some roses, they are just coming to their best now."

"That would be nice, ,dear" answered Margaret, picking up the kitchen scissors. She disappeared into the garden and returned with the beautiful flowers.

They didn't arrive at the church until late in the afternoon, and Stan pulled up behind a battered old Ford Fiesta. As they approached the grave, Margaret suddenly stopped. She felt cold in the early summer sun. "Look, Stan, there's a young woman there," she said, and as they both glanced across the churchyard, their eyes met with those of a pretty young woman, whose hair fell over one side of her face, and on to the collar of a large coat. The young woman made to leave. "Don't go," implored Margaret as she saw the fresh bunch of flowers lying on the grave. "Who are you, don't I know you from somewhere?"

"My name is Hilary Robinson," said the young woman.

Margaret and Stan looked shocked. "Not the Robinsons who moved away fifteen years ago?" asked Stan.

"Yes," came the reply. "Peter and I were at school together, we were friends and we met again in London just one month before his regiment was sent to Afghanistan. I heard of his death when I saw his repatriation on the news."

"If you were a friend of Peter's, then the rift between our families does not concern you, and we thank you for visiting his grave and for mourning him. We had been wondering who it was that was leaving flowers. Let's sit a while together."

As they sat down on the bench, Hilary's coat fell open, and Margaret noticed immediately her swollen belly.

"When is your baby due?" she asked.

"Next week," answered Hilary, "and this is probably the last time I'll be able to come for a while. In case you are wondering, the baby is Peter's. He had asked me to marry him, and we were going to be married when he returned home, but it never happened," and a tear fell from her eyes.

Margaret and Stan were taken aback to discover that they were going to have another grandchild, and Peter's child at that. Stan put his arm around Hilary and Margaret gasped, "Please don't go, come home with us for a while."

They persuaded Hilary to return home with them for tea, and when they found out that she lived alone and was worried how she would support herself and a child they readily suggested that she should stay with them for a time, and see how things worked out. Hilary's eyes filled with tears as she accepted their offer. As Margaret walked back into the living room, having seen Hilary off to return to the small flat she rented, she felt as though she was walking on air.

"Oh Stan, can you believe it? Hilary can have Peter's old room, and we'll have to convert the small bedroom into a nursery!"

So it was that Stan and Margaret spent a large part of the following week emptying the small bedroom of the clutter that they had accumulated over several years. They visited the local DIY shop and bought paint of a pretty pale lemon colour, having asked Hilary If she knew the sex of the baby. She didn't, so the room was decorated in pale lemon, and Margaret got out her old sewing machine and bought material patterned with farmyard animals for new curtains. They also bought a cot, and bed linen, and spring-cleaned Peter's old room. Margaret did her best to give it some feminine touches, and with much sadness managed at last to get rid of some of Peter's old clothes, however they were much too busy to dwell on things.

Although Stan still had to be careful, he was able to drive and they both helped Hilary to move in with them by the end of the week. She was a pleasure to have in their home, and helped Margaret with cooking and other tasks.

After ten days of getting to know one another, at supper one evening Stan asked, "When is this grandchild of mine going to put in an appearance?"

Hilary and Margaret laughed. "He'll come when he's ready," said Margaret. "You know what Peter was like, left everything to the last minute!"

That evening, just as they were getting ready for bed, Hilary knocked on the bedroom door.

"I think the baby's coming, could you drive me to the hospital, Stan?"

"Just try and stop me," said Stan, and both he and Margaret pulled on their clothes.

As they sat in the corridor outside the delivery room Margaret turned to Stan.

"I can't believe we're here. If you had told me even a month ago, I would have said 'don't be silly,' now look at us."

Before Stan could reply, the midwife appeared.

"Would you like to come and meet your new grandson?" she said.

In Pursuit of Happiness

By

Pam Sawyer

Gwen picked up her bags and headed off to the small café in the high street. She ordered a sandwich and coffee and looked around for somewhere to sit. Although it was busy she managed to find an unoccupied table and, waiting for her food, she opened the bag containing the new dress. Feeling its delicate fabric, she became aware of someone standing next to the table.

"Madame, there are no seats available. May I sit here?"

Hardly glancing up, she nodded.

"Lots of bags, you have been shopping?"

"Yes." This time she looked at him. He pointed at the bag containing the dress.

"For a special occasion?"

"Yes, my husband has just been elected captain of his golf club."

"It is a happy occasion, non?"

"Yes, of course."

"Then why are you going to wear black? With your colouring you should be wearing pale blue or lavender."

Not knowing how to reply to this rather personal remark, she was pleased to see the waitress bringing her food. When she looked up at him, he was staring at her.

"Are you in the fashion business, or just rude?"

"My apologies, Madame, I am not in the fashion business, but my late wife was. I cannot get out of the habit of observing ladies; I do not wish to be rude. Let me introduce myself, my name is Eduard Marchant."

He leaned across and shook her hand.

"Your name, Madame?"

"Mrs Horton," she replied rather more tersely than intended, finished her food and coffee and rose from the table.

"Au revoir, Madame, and thank you for letting me share your table."

Arriving home, Gwen took her packages upstairs into her dressing room. Taking the dress out of its bag she held it up against her. Putting it on its hanger she placed it on a hook on the door.

During dinner later, her husband his usual silent self, her thoughts kept turning to the Frenchman. She looked across at Graham. "I have bought a new dress for Saturday evening," she said.

"Did you dear? That's nice, now where is the paper, I'll have coffee in the sitting room."

After loading the dishwasher Gwen took Graham his coffee and, leaving him to his paper, she went upstairs to have another look at the dress.

Next morning, Gwen went back into town and returned the black dress, and tried on several others, including a pale lavender silk shift.

"That really suits you, the colour is great," the sales girl smiled at her and had obviously forgotten her earlier frosty attitude, when Gwen had returned the other dress.

"I'll have it, thank you."

Leaving the shop, Gwen knew she was being rather silly but she went into the café on the off chance that she might see the Frenchman again. He wasn't there and she waited over an hour before leaving and going home. She walked up the street to where her car was parked. As she reached the car she heard a shout: "Madame, Madame Horton!"

Then he was by her side. "I saw you leave the café but you did not see me, tell me, were you looking for me?"

"I think I must have been."

"I see a smile, Madame has a lovely smile."

They started to meet regularly after that, sometimes in the same café at lunchtime, and when the weather was suitable they would take a walk through the park.

A few weeks later Eduard told her that he was returning to France as his work here was almost finished.

He took her hands in his. "Come to France with me."

"I cannot, what about Graham? My life is here, my friends."

"Hah! Graham, does he make you smile? I make you smile, Gwennie, cherie, I can be in your life and be your friend, come with me please." He raised her hands to his lips.

Arriving home, Gwen sat in her car. "Well," she asked herself, "what have I got here? Both the children are married and living abroad, I hardly ever see my grandchildren, and Graham, well I am just a housekeeper and hostess to him. Come on, Gwen, or Gwennie as Eduard calls you, take the bull by the horns."

That night after dinner, carrying the coffee tray into the sitting room, Gwen sat opposite Graham.

"Graham, we need to talk."

"Yes, dear?" he replied still reading his paper.

"I mean seriously, talk." Silence. "Graham, put the bloody paper down!"

"Gwen! Whatever has got into you?"

Gwen took a deep breath, clenched her hands and said, "I'm leaving you."

"You are what?"

"Leaving. I have met someone and I am going to live in France with him."

"What?" he said again. "What nonsense is this? Leaving to live in France? Are you stark raving mad?"

"No, I have never felt saner."

"Who is this someone?" he sneered. "It will be your money, I'll be bound. After all, you're no spring chicken."

"How dare you! He is very wealthy, he runs Marchants, the civil engineering company building the new road tunnel. So my little nest egg will be of no interest to him.

"He's French?"

"Yes!"

"Well then, you have definitely lost your marbles. Is it your hormones or some such rubbish?"

Ignoring his last remark, Gwen stood and made to leave the room. "So, when is this leaving to take place?"

"Tuesday."

"But that's only three days away."

"Yes, I, we are going over on the early ferry crossing, we will be in France for a couple of months and then we plan to do some travelling. I want to go to Texas to see Lizzie, Bob and the children."

"With Johnny Foreigner in tow? Can't see that sitting very well with our daughter, let alone Bob."

"I have spoken to her and she will be pleased to see us." Gwen felt a twinge of guilt at this, as Graham was very fond of Lizzie and was upset when Bob's job took them to America.

"I have arranged for Mrs Jones to come in for an extra day a week, to clean and do some cooking. She will also shop for you, so if you need anything give her a list. And by the way, I am giving her my car."

"What!? Your car?"

"I shan't need it and she has enough trouble walking up the hill from the bus stop, let alone with bags of shopping."

"Got it all planned, haven't you? How long has this been going on?"

"A few months. I am sorry Graham, but we haven't really had much of a life together for years, really since the children left home. Now with you captain at Greenacres, we will have even less time together." Gwen turned and left the room.

The next morning at breakfast Graham informed Gwen that he would be spending the time until she went in one of the guest rooms at the golf club.

Monday night Gwen was all packed. She had given away to charity clothes she would no longer need, although she had carefully packed the lavender silk shift.

Early Tuesday morning, a taxi arrived to take her to the ferry terminal, as it didn't seem right for Eduard to come to the house. The driver took her case and she gave the house and garden one last look, surprised that she felt no regret, just anticipation.

They arrived in France at midday and drove the short distance to Eduard's house. Turning off the main road and into a stony lane, they bumped along the road and round a corner. Eduard stopped the car and pointed.

"We are here."

Gwen looked across to the small house; it was red brick with black wood boards above and a tiled roof. A low garden wall with steps leading directly onto a long, sandy beach surrounded the house. Eduard came round to her side, opened the car door and took her hand.

"Oh, Eduard, it is stunning! Quick, let's go in. I want to see everything."

The next morning Gwen found she was alone in the bed, but there was a delicious smell of coffee. She rose, grabbed her robe and went into the living room. There was no sign of Eduard, just a pot of coffee on the stove.

Going out and down the steps, she walked barefoot across the sand to the sea. She heard a shout.

"Bonjour, Madame!" Eduard was standing on the wall, a long French loaf under one arm. He jumped down and joined her by the water, his free arm round her shoulders.

"How is my Gwennie this morning, happy?"

"More than I can describe."

Gwen thought that happiness for some could be fleeting, but this is probably forever.

Meanwhile across the Channel, Graham was sitting in his spotless kitchen with Mrs Jones on his lap, his arms around her waist, while she fed him freshly baked cupcakes.

Gnome Madness

By

Shelagh O'Grady

Maureen turned the key in the lock and opened the door. To her horror she saw the true extent of her husband's obsession.

"My God, how did it get this bad?" she gasped. "Why didn't I notice it before? Bob must be as mad as a hatter!"

The spacious attic room was lined with shelves and staring at her from every angle were hundreds of garden gnomes. The cheery little fellows with their bulging stomachs, white beards and pointed hats were all grinning at her. Maureen screamed, slammed the door and ran downstairs to the kitchen. Pouring herself a large glass of wine she sank into a chair and took a large gulp. She knew alcohol before breakfast was not a good idea but she was past caring. She wasn't sure how she felt, frightened, angry or disgusted, maybe all three. As the alcohol kicked in she relaxed a little and retraced the events of last night.

Maureen had gone to bed early last night after taking a couple of aspirins for a headache and vaguely remembered Bob clambering in a little later. It was loud banging on the front door which woke her a few hours later. Reaching across to wake Bob she found the bed was empty. Groggy with sleep Maureen pulled on her dressing gown and slippers and went to answer the door.

"Who is it?" she called before slipping off the safety chain.

"It's the police, Mrs Clarke. Can you open the door?"

"What do you want?"

"It's about your husband, Bob Clarke."

Maureen suddenly remembered the empty bed and fear gripped her stomach. Fumbling with the catch she opened the door and saw two police officers standing before her. Drawing her dressing gown around her she stood back.

"You'd better come in."

The two officers stood in the lounge, tall and unsmiling.

"I'm PC Tom Smith and my colleague is WPC Ann Jones. We have a gentleman at the police station we believe to be your husband. Around 1am we received several calls from members of the public reporting that a man was behaving very strangely in the High Street. When we questioned him he became rather abusive, so he has been detained at the police station as a place of safety. He doesn't seem to be drunk but is very agitated." A slight smirk crossed the face of PC Smith whilst WPC Jones stared hard at the floor. Crossing to the mantelpiece PC Smith looked at one of the framed photographs.

"Is this your husband, Mrs Clarke?" he asked.

"Yes, that's Bob. It was taken recently."

"This is the gentleman we have at the station."

"You said he was taken there as a place of safety. What's the matter with Bob?"

The two officers exchanged glances.

"When we found Mr Clarke he was pushing a wheel barrow full of plastic gnomes down the centre of the High Street, standing them along the white line. Although the traffic is quite light at that time of night we were concerned for his safety. When we questioned him he declared that gnomes were going to rule the world and he wanted to make people aware of their existence."

Maureen's eyes pricked with tears as she groped in her dressing gown pocket for a tissue.

"I … I don't know what to say," she replied dabbing her eyes, "I know he likes gnomes and has quite a few around the garden but this is beyond a joke!"

"We'd like you to come with us to the police station. The doctor has been called to assess your husband."

"I need to get dressed first. I can't come in my night clothes," said Maureen, sniffing as she disappeared upstairs.

As Maureen sat in the back of the police car she found the situation quite surreal. The dark, empty streets flew by and her mind seemed to be standing still, unable to function. At the police station she was escorted to the custody suite where she found Bob, accompanied by another police officer in an interview room. As they entered Bob stood up and Maureen stared in horror. He was dressed in a red thigh length tunic, green tights, a red pointed hat and a false beard.

"Bob, what on Earth are you wearing?" Maureen gasped.

"I'm not Bob Clarke. I'm Nobby the Gnome, King of Gnomeland. You will address me as 'Your Majesty'."

Maureen groaned and let out a sob.

"Bob, what's the matter with you? Why are you dressed like that?"

"I've already asked you to address me as 'Your Majesty'. Please don't question my clothing, this is traditional gnome attire."

Maureen felt her knees turn to jelly as WPC Jones guided her to a chair.

"What's happened to him? Why is he behaving like this?" she asked.

"We don't know. The doctor will be here soon. Can I get you a cup of tea?"

"Yes, please, that would be great. Am I safe sitting here? He's not violent is he?"

"I don't think so, but PC Andy Brown will protect you. I won't be a minute."

Maureen sat and gazed at Bob. What had happened? Why was he behaving like this? Where did he find that ridiculous outfit?

"Bob," she said, "please talk to me …"

"Silence!" Bob banged his fist onto the table. "My name is Nobby and I've told you how I'm to be addressed. Bob Clarke is no more! I am Nobby, King of Gnomeland! I and my fellow gnomes are about to take over the world!" he shouted as he stood up and flung his arms into the air.

"Sit down, Sir," said PC Brown. "Don't get too excited."

The door opened and WPC Jones entered carrying a cup of tea. She was followed by an elderly, dishevelled looking gentleman; the doctor, having dressed hurriedly.

"This is Dr Johnstone, er … Your Majesty. He would like a word with you."

"OK," said Nobby. "Please sit down. How can I help you, doctor?"

As Dr Johnstone chatted to Nobby, Maureen sipped her tea.

"I can't stay here listening to this," she said tearfully. WPC Jones led her away to another room.

"What's going to happen to him?" Maureen asked.

"I expect the doctor will admit him to a clinic for a few a days. After that I can't say."

"Can I go home now?" asked Maureen. "I feel so confused."

"I'll drive you back and maybe you could pack an overnight bag for your husband."

Later, with the bag packed and handed to WPC Jones, Maureen closed the front door. In the lounge she sat down and wept.

It was later that morning when she awoke that she went to the attic.

The doctor rang at lunchtime with the news that Bob was to stay at the clinic for six weeks. He wasn't allowed any visitors and perhaps Maureen could stay with family or friends. No longer feeling sad or bewildered Maureen was angry and humiliated. The town was already buzzing with stories of Nobby the gnome as she had discovered when she popped to the shops earlier.

Her anger was boiling into a fury as Maureen marched into the garden armed with Bob's cricket bat. As she lashed out at all the gnome statuettes, heads flew into the bushes, shards of smiling faces beamed up at her from the flower beds and broken pottery littered the lawn. When every figurine had felt the fury of Maureen's anger she stopped and looked around. She felt so much better but she was not finished yet.

Late that afternoon a lorry deposited a large skip in the driveway. Wasting no time Maureen began clearing the garden, loading it with all the pieces of broken pottery, regretting having made such a mess. With the front garden clear she started on the attic. It took a long time and by dusk she had cleared half the room. She sat down feeling tired but satisfied. Tomorrow she would continue with the attic and then there was the shed and the back garden to clear.

Whilst clearing the attic Maureen had found a whole rail of gnome outfits. She planned to put them on a bonfire tomorrow along with the sign "Gnomeland" from the front gate. When, if, Bob came home again there would be no more of this gnome nonsense.

Clearing everything would take several days but she was starting to feel liberated. Clearing away Bob's fantasy was allowing her to find her true self.

Maureen decided to take the doctor's advice and go away. The whispers in the town were increasing so she decided to go and visit her daughter, Lucy, and family in Australia. She hadn't seen them since the grandchildren were tiny as Bob had refused to fly after their plane sustained a bird strike and had made an emergency landing. The grandchildren were now seven and nine and she had missed them growing up. It would also be nice to go somewhere without Bob as he insisted on dominating the conversation with talk about garden gnomes.

Maureen checked the time, 8pm here so about breakfast time in Sydney. Lucy was surprised when her mother rang but delighted when she learnt she was planning to visit. Maureen chose her words carefully, explaining that Bob was in a clinic for a while suffering from a breakdown, and on the doctor's advice Maureen was taking a holiday.

"We'd be delighted to see you Mum, the girls will be so happy to see Nana again. When can we expect you?"

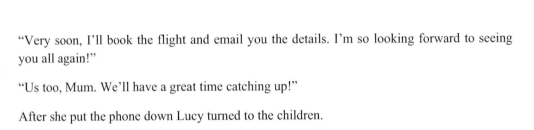

"Very soon, I'll book the flight and email you the details. I'm so looking forward to seeing you all again!"

"Us too, Mum. We'll have a great time catching up!"

After she put the phone down Lucy turned to the children.

"Nana's coming from England to stay for a while. Isn't that great?"

"Is Grampy coming too?"

"No, he's not very well."

"Let's get the garden all tidied up," said Lucy. "We'll have to make sure all the gnomes are looking their best. You know how Nana and Grampy love gnomes!"

Betrayal

By

Angie Simpkins

He turned the key in the lock and opened the door when, to his horror, he saw the green coat hanging on the hallstand. He would never understand what sixth sense had stopped him from calling out his usual, cheery, "I'm home". His heart sank. He felt sick and stumbled forward, undecided what to do. Summoning great presence of mind he slowly reversed, turning quietly as he went back through the door, closing it silently behind him.

How could she do this to him? Again. Barbara had had an affair with Ron's ex-colleague two years before. Alfie, the colleague, had left the firm shortly after and moved away. Barbara had tearfully assured Ron that she was sorry, it was him she really loved and wanted. She had promised that never again would she be unfaithful. Ron realised that the car he had seen parked around the corner, which had looked familiar, was indeed known to him. It was Alfie's beautiful old Jaguar.

Ron got back in his car. Trembling, he started the engine and drove away. He had no plan, no idea where to go. He ended up in the supermarket car park and decided to get a cup of coffee in the café. He sat there, and during the consumption of countless cups of coffee he became more and more angry. How could they do this to him? Especially, how could Barbara, after all she had promised? This time he would not forgive and forget. This time he would get even.

He took out his phone and rang home. "Hello, darling," he heard her say, the lying, cheating bitch, "are you on the way home? I've cooked your favourite meal, I thought we could have a nice, cosy evening in together tonight."

"That would be nice," said Ron, almost choking on the words. "I'll be about an hour." He couldn't believe he could sound so normal, how could Barbara not hear the churning emotions in his voice? He sat a little longer over his coffee and formulated a plan.

That night, when Barbara had gone to sleep, Ron came downstairs, poured himself a glass of whisky and sat for a while, thinking. He remembered that this was the particular brand that Alfie had favoured, perhaps that was why Barbara had chosen to buy it. She usually bought whatever was on offer, and not the more expensive brands. Ron took careful note of the level left in the bottle before he returned to bed.

One week later he again crept downstairs while Barbara was sleeping. Sure enough, the level on the whisky bottle had fallen, confirming Ron's suspicions. He took the small bottle he had purchased from a dubious character he had been introduced to by his boss, Doug. Doug had never liked Alfie, especially when Alfie had left and taken all his clients with him to his new firm. Doug had had difficulty explaining that away to the owner of the company. Ron poured himself a small glass of whisky. "Might as well, won't be able to have any more," he thought as he topped up the bottle with the contents of the small bottle.

It was ten days later when Ron noticed the news flash on the board outside the local newsagent – "Local businessman found dead in his car." Ron bought the paper and opened it out to read, "Local businessman, Alfred Hopkins, was found slumped at the wheel of his old Jaguar at the entrance to Manley Park. He was taken to City Hospital but was declared dead on arrival. The police are investigating his death."

Ron threw the paper away, with a small, satisfied smile, and went home.

"I'm home," he called out cheerily as he entered the hall. He heard a noise from the living room. "Hello, darling," he said, entering the room. "Whatever's the matter? You look upset." Barbara was sitting on the sofa watching one of her soaps on the television.

"Oh, hello," she said with a sniffle, "it's a very sad story."

"You silly little bunnykins," said Ron, sitting down next to her and putting his arm around her. "It's only TV, it's not real life. Why don't I pour you a glass of whisky to buck you up?"

Where Is It?

By

Pam Corsie

He turned the key in the lock and opened the door. To his horror he saw the safe was empty.

"What has happened?" he mumbled.

"What do you mean, what has happened?"

The man in the full-face balaclava shoved Michael to one side. "Where is it?" he shouted. "Where's the cash? What have you done with it?"

"I, I haven't done anything with it," stammered Michael. "I don't know where it is. It should be here. I only locked it up just after eight when we closed. My boss is going to kill me!"

"Your boss is the least of your worries, by the time I've finished with you there'll not be much left for him to do anything with."

"Please don't hurt me," Michael grovelled from the corner of the room where the would-be robber had trapped him. "Please don't hurt me."

The robber was sweating profusely and damp patches were forming in the armpits of his T-shirt and down the centre of his chest. Perhaps he's scared too, thought Michael. It was difficult to judge his age as his face was covered by the balaclava but his body was agile and he moved constantly from one foot to the other, backwards and forwards, always in front of Michael, never letting his guard drop and never giving Michael the chance to make a run for the door.

The robber was getting agitated and Michael was very nervous about the way he brandished the pistol. He had never seen a gun in real life, not even in a display case. Being so close to one now was terrifying. Even if he was brave enough to have a go at getting it off the robber and he didn't get shot in the process, he wouldn't know how to use it. He'd watched films about hostage situations, for this was how he now felt – a hostage. He knew about safety catches on guns. If it wasn't on, there was every chance he'd be shot trying to wrestle the gun away and, if it was on, he didn't know how to get it off so he could shoot the robber.

Who was he kidding? He didn't think his wobbly legs would sustain an attack on the robber and an escape bid on all fours was never going to work. Michael was a clever chap, too bright for a general factotum job in a builders' merchants, but that had been the only work he could get when he was sent down from Oxford, with a half-finished degree and a criminal conviction for buying and selling illegal substances. Perhaps he wasn't as clever as he thought he was.

"What's your name?" he asked the sweating, agitated robber.

"What do you want to know that for?"

"We are going to be stuck together for a while, I don't want to call you 'Oi'. My name is Michael, Mike to my friends."

"We ain't friends, we ain't nuffin."

"Please yourself."

The nameless robber continued to pace the room anxiously, pointing the gun at Michael from time to time. "Where's the money?" he shouted, crouching over his hostage and shoving the gun into Michael's throat. "Where is it, you snooty, stuck-up, jerk?"

Michael tried to swallow but the gun pressing on his larynx made it a painful experience and he waved his arms in an attempt to get the robber to move back. He recoiled from Michael briefly, revealing a soaking wet back to his filthy T-shirt. He could be as scared as me, thought Michael, or desperate for a fix. During his brief career as a purveyor of illegal substances he had witnessed a few of his clients' suffering as they waited for him to produce the goods or as they plummeted to new depths coming down from something they had taken. The robber was beginning to fit the mould.

"What do you want the money for?" asked Michael.

"Nuffin' to do with you."

"Drugs?"

"Mind your own business."

"Come on, Rob. Yes, that's what I'll call you, Rob, short for robber. You can tell me."

"Call me what you like but I ain't telling you nuffin'."

"It'll only get worse, Rob. The sweats, then the pain will set in, the cramps in your fingers and toes, the gnawing feeling in your gut, the maggots feeding on your brain. It'll only get worse."

"Shuttup, bleeding posh boy, what do you know about anyfink?"

"You'd be surprised what I know, very surprised indeed, I think."

"What's a Nob like you doing working in a place like this?"

By now Michael's confidence was returning and he watched with some sympathy as Rob's body started to forsake him. The jitters were becoming more pronounced, the sweat was pouring from under the balaclava, he couldn't keep still and he continued to wave the gun about.

Michael slowly raised himself into a crouched position.

"Don't get any stupid ideas, Nob."

"I won't, but my legs were dead underneath me. I just want to get my circulation moving again. I promise I won't do anything. Look, my hands are pressed against the wall as I try to stand here. I'll leave them where you can see them. No sudden movements, I promise, Rob."

"Ha ha, Rob, Nob! I'm a poet." Rob went off into peals of manic laughter that culminated in a body wracking coughing fit, but never let go of the pistol.

My luck will run out soon, thought Michael. I need to get him on my side, befriend him. Outside, through the office window he could see the black sky and twinkling stars. It was getting late. His mother would be worried that he had not gone straight home. He would be breaking his curfew if he didn't clock in soon.

"Hey, Rob! Have you seen one of these?" asked Michael rolling up the leg of his jeans to reveal a tag.

"What did you do to get that?" Rob's voice took on a touch of admiration. He didn't have a tag although a lot of his mates did.

So Michael explained about being at uni, the pressure to achieve having gone from the local grammar school into an environment where everyone seemed to be brighter, harder working and more successful than he was. He had started with uppers to keep himself awake at night so he could finish assignments and then came downers to bring him back to normality in the morning. For the spring term this had been a workable pattern but after the Easter break he needed more and more and eventually started selling to other students in the same situation so that he could finance his own habit.

All through the second year he had managed to keep his guilty secret but in the October following the summer vacation he had to find a new supplier. He found himself the victim of a honey trap set by fellow students and he was encouraged to hand himself over to the police. Charges followed, a court case and sentencing. "And that's how I got the tag, sent down from Oxford and my probation officer found me this dead-end job."

During Michael's confession Rob had slumped in the chair behind the desk, the gun still in his hand, still pointing at Michael. With his left hand he had pulled off the balaclava and revealed a pale, spotty face with dull eyes surrounded by deep grey rings. "I almost like you," he whispered. "I thought you were a Nob, and you still are, but at least you are a Nob who has some idea what normal people have to go through."

"I need to get home before 10 p.m., Rob. If I break the terms of my parole I'll be in deep trouble. Why don't you go and I'll call the law and tell them you legged it. Here's twenty quid, that should see you right till the morning."

Rob didn't move.

"Alright, alright, forty quid. That's all I've got."

Rob's need for a fix overcame him and he snatched the notes from Michael's outstretched hand. He turned, shoved the gun behind the belt in the back of his jeans and shot out of the office door.

The police responded quickly to Michael's 999 call.

"Well, Officer, I was just locking the staff exit door on my way out after we closed when this kid shoved a gun in my back and told me to come back in and open the safe."

"What sort of kid? What did he look like? How old was he?"

"I didn't see his face, he was wearing a balaclava. I guess about my age, scruffy, sweaty. I called him Rob."

"You'd better come down to the station, make a statement."

Michael showed the officer his tag. "I've got to be home by 10 or I'll be in big trouble. You can't take me to the station."

"We can, and we will. I'll call your probation officer and explain. We'll even give you a ride home after the statement so no chance of getting into more trouble."

It was after midnight when Michael finally got home. His mum was waiting for him with a cup of hot chocolate and a dried-out roast dinner. "Thanks a lot," he grunted as he ignored the dinner and took the hot chocolate up to his room.

At the builders' merchants the next morning, Michael was greeted kindly by everyone, even those who had not deigned to speak to him previously. He was patted on the shoulder and given man hugs by concerned colleagues. He enjoyed the attention but played it very coyly.

"I'll lock up tonight, Mike," said the boss that evening as he waved Michael off the shop floor.

"I'll just get my bag and I'll be off," replied Michael as he went into the deserted staff locker room. As he took his rucksack from the secure locker, before he slung it across his back, he couldn't resist a glance inside at yesterday's £10,760 takings. He thanked his lucky stars that, as he was returning last night to collect it, that idiot had tried to rob the place. Now he had the money and nobody suspected him at all.

Local Man Dies in Brawl

By

Pam Sawyer

He turned the key in the lock and to his horror saw the local newspaper with its stark headline lying on the mat. Ben picked up the paper and, closing the door with his foot, he started to read.

Alex Masters, a student aged 21, was involved in a fight with some youths when he was knocked to the ground and hit his head. He died instantly. The police are trying to trace a young man who was a witness to the fight but left the area before Alex Masters fell.

Ben sat down heavily on the kitchen chair with his head in his hands. Just three short days ago their lives had changed forever.

He would never forget the agonised cry from his mother when the police came and gave his parents the news, the look on his father's face, tears filling his eyes. Ben had tried to put his arms around his mother to comfort her but she pushed him away. Both his parents barely spoke to him over the next few weeks. Then finally Alex's body was released and Ben and his parents were able to arrange the funeral.

At the wake after the ceremony Ben was cornered by his aunt Diana.

"Well, young man, what are your plans?"

"I don't know. Mum and Dad seem to resent me being here instead of Alex. I'm a failure in their eyes."

"Nonsense. OK, so Alex was a bit of a star."

"Huh, a bit of a star? A first at Cambridge, all set for a glittering career in the law. Then there's me who couldn't even get decent enough A-levels to get me into uni."

"Well, we can't all be high fliers. Get out in the world and make something of yourself, lad."

"Like what?"

"Well, have you saved any cash from your holiday jobs?"

"Some, I was hoping to buy a car. Why?"

"Get away from here for a while. Clear off abroad."

"Leave Mum and Dad? A bit harsh isn't it?"

"You said they are somewhat hostile towards you at the moment. Go and work away for a few months."

Ben thought about his aunt's suggestion and came to the conclusion she was probably right. A couple of weeks later he took a ferry to France and then hitch-hiked his way down to Spain. His last ride dropped him off on the outskirts of Barcelona by a roadside bar. Using the little Spanish he knew, Ben enquired if there was anywhere he could stay. The barman waved him to a table and went through a tatty beaded curtain. Ben could hear a babble of Spanish. A middle-aged woman appeared and made her way to Ben's table.

"Hi. Miguel tells me you are looking for somewhere to stay."

"Yes. Are you English?"

"I am and I have rooms here. How long do you want to stay?"

"Well, a few days at least. I shall be looking for work."

"Any bar experience? If so, you can start here. Miguel is leaving this coming Saturday."

"Well, I worked in my local pub back in England but I don't have much Spanish."

"No worries, you will soon get the hang of it. It's quite simple here, nearly all locals. They have the same thing to drink most nights. Now, I'm Liz. Who are you?"

This was to become a life-changing time for Ben. He worked in the bar at night and during the day he started doing repair jobs around the place. He replaced the tatty beaded curtain and repaired a couple of tables he found out the back of the bar. He tidied up the rear paved space and suggested to Liz that it would make an extra seating area and perhaps the tables he had fixed could do with a lick of paint then they could go out there. Liz was impressed with him and asked him if he minded doing some painting and decorating of the three rooms she let.

So Ben's life took on a whole new meaning. He did telephone home a couple of times. His parents didn't seem to miss him. He also spoke to his aunt Diana who told him that three young men had been arrested in connection with Alex's death. But they were still looking for the young man who may have witnessed what happened.

Ben was enjoying his life in Spain. His Spanish improved and he and Liz had a good working relationship. One afternoon when the bar closed for the siesta, Ben was making his way upstairs to his room when Liz appeared. She was holding two glasses. She took Ben's hand and led him into her bedroom. She put the glasses down and took a bottle of Cava from a small fridge. Handing the bottle to Ben she motioned for him to open it. He stared at Liz with a puzzled look on his face.

"Don't be shy, Ben, pour us both a glass."

After that, Ben spent every afternoon with Liz. Later they would take a shower together and then re-open the bar at six o'clock. This arrangement went on for several months and Ben decided life was so good here in Spain he had no intention of returning to the UK.

One morning Ben was dealing with a delivery for the bar when he went fetch Liz to pay the driver. He was surprised she hadn't appeared as she was usually up early. He went up to her room and tapped on the door. There was no reply so he tapped harder. When she didn't answer he called her name as he opened the door. Liz was sprawled on the floor still in her night clothes. Ben felt for a pulse; there was nothing. He knelt beside her, taking her still-warm hand.

"Oh Liz, my lovely Liz."

Tears streamed down his face. Ben left her where she was and went downstairs where the delivery man was waiting. He pointed to the stairs and the man hurried up them. He came back down and telephoned the emergency services on his mobile while shaking his head at Ben.

Ben was distraught. He didn't open the bar that day or the next. Liz's patrons, neighbours and friends all called, leaving flowers at the bar.

A few days later Liz's solicitor called. He told Ben that Liz had made plans for her funeral and that she wanted it to take place in the UK. Ben asked if he could accompany her back to England and make sure her wishes were carried out. The solicitor agreed and told Ben that he was to go to a firm of solicitors in Guildford, where Liz came from, and he would be given the instructions that she had left.

Sitting in the crematorium waiting for the ceremony to begin, Ben looked around. He counted 15 people. They all stood as the coffin was carried in. Ben was surprised to hear the music chosen. All three songs were ones that he and Liz had enjoyed together, often playing them in the bar.

Ben realised that Liz must have planned this since they met. He felt a lump rise in his throat as the last song was played. How he regretted that he had never told her that he loved her. After the service, Ben hurried away as he remembered that he had to go back to the solicitor. He drove into Guildford in his hire car. Finding a place to park, he walked down the street with his thoughts full of memories of Liz and how much he was going to miss her. Perhaps this was the time for him to move on. He was ushered into the office of the same man as he had seen before.

"Well, Mr Masters, please sit. I have some news for you regarding Mrs Elizabeth Jacobs' estate."

Ben sat down as the man shuffled some papers.

"Mrs Jacobs has left you the bulk of her estate. There are a few personal items she has left to friends and distant relatives. The rest is for you, Mr Masters."

Ben was stunned, he couldn't speak. He heard the man's voice but couldn't take in what was being said.

"So, do you understand, Mr Masters? Mrs Jacobs' properties here and in Spain are worth somewhere in the region of £300,000. Plus about £50,000 cash after various expenses have been dealt with."

Ben was in shock.

"Any questions, Mr Masters?"

"No, I don't think so. I just don't understand."

"Mrs Jacobs was obviously very fond of you. Now, will you be going back to Spain? We will need to contact you when probate has been granted."

"Yes, I think so. I have one or two matters to deal with here and then I will go back."

Ben collected the car and drove the 40 miles to his parents' house, his thoughts still reeling from the news he had received.

He parked the car in the drive and rang the bell. A short time passed and then his mother opened the door.

She didn't speak, just pulled him into her arms.

"Ben, oh son, come in."

Ben followed his mother into the house. Holding his hand, she led him into the sitting room. His father was sitting reading the paper. He stood and reached for Ben's hand. Ben wasn't surprised to see how both had aged as his mother bustled about offering tea.

Ben sat down with his parents and told them what he had been doing since he left all those months ago.

"Are you back for the trial, son?" his father asked. "Do you know the three lads charged with Alex's death? The police are still looking for the other lad who wasn't involved but may have witnessed the fight."

"No, Dad. I have to get back to Spain. The bar is closed for a week or so. But I have staff who are relying on me, I can't let them down, and no, I don't recognise the names of the three involved."

"Well, you certainly fell on your feet with that woman."

"Yes, I have been very lucky. I just wish you could have met Liz, she was a lovely lady."

Ben felt the familiar lump in his throat as he thought of Liz. He rose and took the tray of tea things out to the kitchen. His mother hugged him.

"Where you going now?"

"There is something I have to do before I get ready to leave."

"Come back here, sleep here in your old room."

Ben hesitated briefly.

"OK, I'll be back hopefully within the hour."

Ben drove off, parked his car and walked up the steps to the door of the police station.

Acknowledgements

Angie, Pam C, Pam S and Shelagh would like to thank their families who have been, for the most part, supportive and encouraging during the writing and production of this anthology. Special thanks must go to Karen of KS Editing who has proofread everything we have written and offered lots of advice, help and support. She has generously shared her knowledge, experience and time to make this anthology reach a professional looking conclusion and we are all very grateful.

Angie, Pam S and Shelagh would also like to express their thanks to Pam C whose enthusiasm, energy and hard work has made this project actually happen.